PINEAPPLE LAND WAR

A Pineapple Port Mystery: Book Four

Amy Vansant

ISBN-13: 978-1543166392
ISBN-10: 1543166393
Library of Congress: 2017902954

Vansant Creations, LLC / Amy Vansant
Annapolis, MD
http://www.AmyVansant.com
http://www.PineapplePort.com

Copy editing by Carolyn Steele.
Proofreading by Effrosyni Moschoudi & Connie Leap
Cover by Steven Novak

DEDICATION

To my dad, the original Captain Ron, who loved the idea of a guy stuck to the end of a mast, and I love that about him.

CHAPTER ONE

William "Bucky" Bloom leaned against the roof deck railing, staring down at his enormous sailboat in the marina below. He liked to enjoy his evenings away from home with a view of the Gulf of Mexico and a glass of Scotch.

Or four.

Arms encircled his waist, and he jumped with surprise, sloshing a mouthful of Scotch twenty stories down to the decks below.

His girlfriend, Shawna, moved like a cat. He found it unnerving.

"Where are we going for dinner, sexy?" she asked.

He twisted his neck to glare at her. "Don't sneak up on me. You'll give me a heart attack."

"You're not going to have a heart attack. You're as strong as a bull." She reached down and rested her cupped hand on his little *bull,* and he offered her a wistful smile.

She was lying about his sexual prowess. At sixty-seven years old, he was lucky to feel anything stirring down there but the urge to pee. He needed help from pharmaceuticals to achieve much more, but he did appreciate her flattery. That was their unspoken agreement, after all—he provided material gifts, and she made him feel young again.

He shooed her away. "All right, enough of that. We'll go to the Sundowner for dinner. Go get ready."

She stepped beside him and leaned over the railing, arms outstretched. The diamond bracelet he'd bought her a week before glimmered beneath the setting sun.

"Look! I'm queen of the world!"

"Get down off of there." He jerked the waistband of her yoga tights, and she stumbled back, giggling, before scampering off to dress for dinner.

Bucky took the last sip of his Scotch and closed his eyes.

The younger my mistresses, the more annoying.

And expensive.

Maybe it was time to find someone closer to his age.

Maybe thirty.

Eh.

Maybe twenty-somethings were fine. He just needed one with a little more sophistication. Like that feisty blonde, he was still determined to get—*that one was a tease.*

* * *

"Go mind the bow line."

Barb glared at her husband as he motioned to her from behind the wheel of their forty-two-foot Farr cruising sailboat. The Farr was too much boat for Lyle. Barb told him as much two or three times an outing. Yet here they were, screaming at each other *again* as he frantically attempted to dock the damn thing.

A relaxing end to an equally relaxing day of wrestling with sails and jibs and whatever the rest of the crap hanging off this stupid boat is. Barb gritted her teeth and vowed to sink the thing, an oath she swore at the end of every trip.

She shimmied toward the bow as the dock loomed into view. *I should be somewhere sipping a cocktail if it wasn't for this—*

A low *boom!* cut Barb's thought short. Something flashed in her peripheral vision. She swiveled her attention toward the marina apartment building and squinted, but whatever she'd seen was gone. *Probably a bird.* All she saw now was the bobbing sailboat docked adjacent to the residence tower, the aptly named *Landlubber*. It was always docked; she'd never seen it leave—

Wait.

Something odd was mounted at the top of the *Landlubber*'s mast.

Had a heron swooped in and perched there?

No...the object appeared connected to the side of the mast.

Some sort of sonar? But so oddly shaped. Something about it—

She gasped.

That's not a sonar. That's a—

Her husband plowed their sailboat into the pier. Distracted by the *Landlubber*'s mast, the sudden jolt tossed her forward without resistance, her face narrowly missing a piling as she tumbled, legs and arms akimbo, grasping for anything that might stop her fall. Her hip clipped the edge of the dock, and she ping-ponged from the dock to the boat to the water.

A moment later, she surfaced, sputtering.

"Barb!" Lyle stared down at her from the side of the boat, his face twisted with anger. "What the hell are you doing? You have to pay attention—"

"The sailboat," she said, pointing with a broken nail.

Lyle rolled his eyes. "Oh, right. It's the *boat's* fault you fell."

She slapped the water in frustration and swam to the ladder at the end of the pier. Scrambling to the top, she continued to jab a finger in the direction of the *Landlubber*, eyes locked on its mast. She needed to know she hadn't dreamt it. Rubbing her bruised hip, she spotted the object that had distracted her from her duties.

Ha.

She turned to Lyle and snapped her arm like a whip, pointing. "Not *our* sailboat, you jackass; the one by the residences. Look at the mast."

Lyle tracked her gesture, his gaze tracing the line of the *Landlubber*'s mast upward.

Something of interest caused his chin to cease rising. His head tilted to the right, eyes narrowing and neck craning forward like a zoom lens.

"Do you see it?" asked Barb.

Lyle's jaw fell. "Is that—?"

She nodded. "You *do* see it."

She wasn't crazy. Those were *legs* bent at the knee, arms splayed on either side, head lolled back, mouth opened wide as if the man were trying to catch rain.

She hadn't dreamed it.

A *man* was impaled on the top of the *Landlubber's* mast.

"But how—" Lyle stopped short as his chin began to rise again.

Barb's gaze shot to the tower's rooftop deck as a young woman with long dark hair appeared at the railing and stared down at the skewered man.

Lyle looked at Barb. "Did she push him?"

She shrugged. "I don't know. But makes you think maybe you should be nicer to me, doesn't it?"

The young woman shrieked.

CHAPTER TWO

"Did you hear?"

Penny threw her swim bag onto a lounge chair and wrestled out of her hibiscus-print cover-up, elbows poking everywhere.

"You missed water aerobics," said Darla, climbing the pool stairs with Mariska and Charlotte on her heels.

"Yeah, it was a good one, too," said Charlotte. They'd done water aerobics to the same tape for three years. Her comment was sarcastic, but the chances anyone would notice were slim.

"Oh, it *was* a good one," said Mariska.

Case in point.

"Forget that nonsense," snapped Penny. Penny's disdain for water aerobics bordered on pathological. It was as if her whole family had been killed in a freak water aerobics accident. The only time she participated was when she felt like she'd fallen behind on neighborhood gossip because Pineapple Port aerobics involved a lot more yapping than swimming.

"You look like you're bustin' at the seams to share something," said Darla, squinting at her.

Penny nodded. "I am. Bucky's dead."

The others stared at her with blank expressions.

"I knew someone with a cat named Bucky," said Mariska after a moment.

"Bucky's your cat?" Charlotte asked Penny.

Penny's expression twisted with what appeared to be disgust. "Why would I get a *cat*?"

"Bucky would be a good name for a hamster," said Darla.

"Or a rabbit," chimed Mariska.

Penny huffed. "You idiots. Bucky *Bloom* is dead."

Mariska gasped. "No. How?"

"Probably overdosed on Viagra, horny old dirtball," said Darla, reaching for her towel.

Penny shook her head so violently that Charlotte feared she might lift off like a helicopter. "No. That was my first guess, too, but he fell onto the mast of a sailboat. Can you believe it?"

"You mean he hit his head on it?" asked Darla.

"No, he *fell on it*. Fell off the rooftop deck of his marina sex pad right on to the mast."

"*On to it*?" echoed Charlotte, poking her finger into her flattened palm.

"Like a cocktail olive." An enormous grin spread across Penny's face.

Charlotte immediately knew something was up. Penny was never that happy about anything.

As the owner of the Pineapple Port fifty-five-plus retirement community, Penny *had* been kind enough to allow Charlotte to remain after her grandmother—who'd served as her guardian after her parents' death—had died. Other than that unusual stroke of benevolence, Charlotte couldn't think of a single thing the community's matriarch had ever done to warm the cockles of anyone's heart.

Still, the sheer *width* of the smile plastered on her face as she told the sad tale of a man impaled on a sailboat mast...that was warped, even for her. Penny's ears were about to shake hands on the back of her head.

"Why do I get the impression Bucky's death benefits you somehow? Or do you just have a thing for a good skewering?"

Mariska winced. "*Skewering*. Oh my. What a word. This is terrible."

"Bucky owns Cow Town," said Darla before Penny could answer. Penny nodded and clapped her fingers together with glee.

Cow Town. That explained it. Cow Town was a piece of land on the outskirts of Pineapple Port that Penny and her husband, George, had wanted to buy for as long as anyone could remember. The owner—who Charlotte now knew was Bucky Bloom—rented it as grazing land for cows, probably waiting for the tract to become even more valuable.

If the owner of the land was dead, Penny finally had a chance to grab it.

"Have you talked to Cora?" asked Darla.

Penny snorted with disdain. "*That* idiot. I'm not worried about her. Her husband's body was found by his twenty-seven-year-old mistress, the last in a string of who knows how many. Everyone knew what a cheater he was except her. She's a *moron.*"

"How did he fall?" asked Mariska.

"Who knows? Probably drunk."

"Does Pussy Galore know yet?" asked Darla.

Charlotte watched the blood drain from Penny's face.

"Oh, I don't know."

Penny grabbed her cover-up, shimmied her collection of bones back into it and snatched her swim bag from the chair. She ran from the pool area without another word.

Charlotte turned to Darla. "Does she always run away when people mention James Bond girls? Isn't that something you should have told me a long time ago? It could have come in handy."

Darla wrapped her towel around her waist. "Pussy Galore owns Silver Lake. She wants Cow Town every bit as much as Penny does for all the same reasons...expansion."

"They're slum lords," said Mariska. She giggled and then slapped her hand over her mouth, eyes darting toward their water aerobics leader, Jackie, whose late husband had been an *actual* slum lord. "Whoops."

Charlotte chuckled. "I'm going to hate myself for asking, but is this woman's *real* name Pussy Galore?"

"No. Her name is Tabitha, and she goes by Tabby, like the

cat. Somewhere, years ago, Penny started calling her Pussy Galore, and it stuck."

"Does she know about this nickname?"

"She knows, but she doesn't like it."

"I can't imagine why."

Charlotte had an odd feeling and paused to put her finger on the cause of it.

Ah. Silence.

Chatter, growing to a healthy din around the pool since the beginning of water aerobics, had stopped as if someone had cut the gossip faucet. She peered down the line of the Olympic-sized pool and found all gazes pointed behind her.

She turned to find her boyfriend, Declan, walking towards her, towel casually thrown over his square shoulders. His swimmer's body was visible, broad-chested and tapering at the waist. He had abs like the underside of a turtle shell. He smiled, and she swore she could hear the retired ladies sigh in unison behind her.

"Hello, everyone. How are you?" he asked.

"Surrounded by a bunch of randy old ladies, apparently," mumbled Charlotte as he pecked her on the cheek and shook hands with Mariska and Darla.

"What brings you here?" asked Charlotte.

Before he could answer, Darla interjected.

"I'm so glad you decided to take me up on my invite to use the pool."

Charlotte scowled. "Hey, I've invited you a million times, and you've never come."

He shrugged. "I decided my lap pool can get pretty boring." He strolled toward a chair to set his towel on it and called back to Charlotte. "Darla said today was the day to come."

"Today?"

One of the ladies who had been on the opposite side of the pool a moment earlier bumped into Darla as she passed. Charlotte spotted her slide cash into Darla's hand as she passed, grinning at Declan with eyes so flirty that Charlotte thought her lashes might flit away and mate with the nearest butterfly.

Charlotte gasped. "Darla! You pimp!"

Darla's mouth contracted into the shape of an *O*. "Missy, I'm sure ah don't know whut you're talkin' about." Her Southern accent always became more pronounced when she was lying.

"What's in your hand?" Charlotte demanded to know.

Darla held out an empty palm. "Nothin'?"

"The other one."

She unrolled her clenched fist, revealing a crumpled five-dollar bill. "Oh, that? Patty owed me money from the, uh, last bake sale."

Mariska cocked her head. "From the last bake sale? You said Patty offered you five dollars to get Declan here without his shirt—"

Darla cut Mariska short, nearly shouting to drown out her friend. "That's right. I did talk to her about a *darling* shirt that I thought would look good on Declan."

Charlotte shook her head. "You ladies are awful. And as for Panting Patty—" She turned and saw Patty had moved to the fence, studying Declan from a new angle.

"Did I miss something?" asked Declan, returning his attention to the group.

Charlotte sighed. "Maybe. But Patty isn't missing a *thing*."

"Charlotte!" Penny came pounding back into the pool area, grabbed Charlotte by the wrist, and began dragging her toward the parking lot.

Charlotte planted her feet to stop the momentum. "What are you doing?"

"You're coming with me."

"Why?"

"Because I have to go talk to Cora before Pussy gets to her and—"

"I really wish you would stop saying that—"

"—and I just remembered she *loves* orphan kids. Cooks orphan kids porridge in her free time or some such crap."

"What's that got to do with me?"

"You're an orphan."

"But I'm twenty-six years old."

"Close enough. Plus, I want you to suss out my best angle. Maybe help me find some dirt on Pussy."

"Ew." *That was even more horrific.*

"You don't understand. I *need* you there from the get-go. *I'm hiring you.*"

"Oh." Charlotte flashed a smile back at the group and allowed Penny to lead her toward the gate. "Why didn't you say so?"

CHAPTER THREE

"Just so you know, I don't have my detective license yet," said Charlotte as Penny pulled up in front of a large ranch-style home on the outskirts of Cow Town.

Penny scoffed. "So what? Just keep your ears and eyes open for opportunity."

Charlotte straightened the colorful, frilly-edged shirt tickling her neck. Penny had dragged her into her *own home* and picked out the most juvenile thing in her closet. At least the frantic woman had given her time to change. For a moment, she thought her first conversation with the widow Cora Bloom would be in a wet bathing suit.

"Don't you think I should have worn something a little less festive to visit a new widow?"

Penny shook her head. "No. I want you to look as orphan-y as possible."

"Orphan-y? You should have said so. I would have worn my curly red Annie wig."

"You have one?"

"No."

"Hm."

Penny slithered out of her white Cadillac as gracefully as possible in the form-fitting and more appropriate black skirt-suit into which she'd changed. She opened the back door to retrieve a large flower arrangement.

As she struggled with the lilies, Charlotte stepped out and watched another large, white Cadillac park behind them. A tan, bony, older woman in an identical black skirt-suit emerged and opened the back door of *her* car. She leaned in and jerked a huge colorful flower arrangement into the sun, like a never-ending parade of clowns spilling from her car.

Penny straightened, lilies in hand, and closed her back door with her foot. As soon as her gaze fell on the other woman, she froze, and the two of them stood that way, arms wrapped around impossibly large flower arrangements, staring through the foliage like rival gorillas.

Each possessed similar helmet-shaped hair, hawk-noses, and bodies like x-rays.

"I always wondered what the twins from *The Shining* looked like all grown up," mumbled Charlotte.

"Hello, *Penelope*," said the woman after several seconds.

Penny's lip twitched. "Hello, *Pussy*."

The woman snarled. "I told you not to call me that, you miserable—"

"Uh, do you want me to take that, Penny?" offered Charlotte holding out her arms.

Penny's attention snapped to her, returned to Tabby, and then swiveled toward the front door of the rancher. Tabby, too, pointed her gaze to the Bloom residence. They both took one last glance at each other and began powerwalking toward the house, identical low-heeled, dark pumps wobbling on the uneven pavers as they shifted and re-shifted their flower arrangements to keep from veering into the shrubbery.

Charlotte scurried after them.

The women jockeyed for position at the door, sword fighting with their flowers. Petals abandoned hope that they might spread joy and fluttered to the ground to die.

A small woman in a dark navy Mumu opened the door. She craned her neck to see the faces behind the flower.

"Penny, Tabby. What a surprise. How are my favorite twins?"

Charlotte looked at the two women with fresh eyes. *They*

really are twins. That explains a lot.

"Cora, you dear thing. I was so sorry to hear about your loss," said Penny.

"*So* sorry," echoed Tabby.

"It was quite a shock. Please, come inside."

Both women jostled forward, bouncing between the door jamb and each other's arrangements. Tabby grunted and shoved forward into the foyer with Penny on her heels.

Charlotte spotted a flash of red as someone wearing Louboutin shoes slipped out of the hall and into what looked like the kitchen beyond. Another person sharing sympathies, no doubt. She felt bad that someone who had just lost their husband would have to field so many guests and tried to look as small as possible.

It didn't work. Cora's gaze fell upon her.

"Who are you?" she asked.

"I'm Charlotte—"

"She's my orphan!" yelped Penny as she set her flowers on the floor. Her bony spine poked at the back of her suit like that of an underfed Stegosaurus.

"Your orphan?" asked Cora, taking Charlotte's fingers in her own soft, crêpey hand.

"She found me in a box of Cracker Jack," said Charlotte.

Penny made a noise somewhere between a laugh and a growl. "Isn't she funny? Her grandmother lived in Pineapple Port, and I let her stay after she died. The grandmother, that is, not Charlotte. Charlotte's still alive. Of course. She's right here. I practically raised her."

Penny's eyes flashed, daring Charlotte to contradict her.

Cora's hand fluttered to her heart. "Why, that's wonderful, Penny. I had no idea. You know, I work with the orphans in Tampa."

Penny released a surprised gasp, securing herself the Oscar for the visit. "Do you? Isn't that *wonderful*. Though certainly not a surprise to hear. You've always been so kind-hearted."

Tabby stood behind Penny, staring laser holes through the back of her head. "Penny, I forget—was that before or after they found that woman's bones in Pineapple Port?"

Penny's face drained of color.

"What's that now?" asked Cora.

"Nothing, nothing dear—"

A woman in a maroon, utilitarian housekeeper's dress appeared in the hallway. "Ma'am, can I get anything for you and your guests?"

Cora's eyes darted to the kitchen. "Uh—"

Tabby and Penny looked at each other as Cora stalled. Charlotte knew each wanted to corner the widow alone in order to state their case for buying Cow Town. Neither wanted to broach the subject with the other there. Sharing food together would be a waste of time.

"We don't want to take up any more of your time—just wanted to offer our condolences. We'll get out of your hair," said Tabby.

Penny agreed, and the housekeeper wandered off with a nod.

"Well, it was lovely of you to stop by. Especially since I'll be leaving soon."

The sisters' eyes grew large, and the women stopped their progress toward the door as if they'd smacked into a wall.

"Leaving?" asked Penny.

Cora nodded and opened the front door, ushering them through it. "I'm going to live with our son in Connecticut."

Tabby smiled. "How wonderful for you. So, you'll be selling this lovely house?"

"Yes. And all the land."

"To *whom*?" said Penny before she could stop herself.

Cora positioned herself inside the door and blinked at the women now standing on her porch.

"That depends on you two, doesn't it?"

The twins drew a collective gasp.

"You want our best bid?" asked Tabby.

The widow Bloom's eyes narrowed, and a smile slithered across her lips, instantly transforming her from the kindly old widow-lady into a crone offering tasty apples to Snow White.

This just got interesting.

Charlotte felt like an innocent victim about to die along with the intended targets.

"Oh, I don't want your best bid," Cora said, pausing for dramatic effect before continuing. "But I do want you to *pay*."

"I don't understand. Are you saying you're not selling to us?" asked Tabby.

"I'm definitely selling to one of you. Nobody wants my land more than you two vultures."

"But you don't want bids?" asked Penny.

"Sixty-nine and eighty-eight."

The twins looked at each other to see if the other understood Cora's cryptic message.

Penny took the lead. "What's sixty-nine and eighty-eight? Your price? I don't understand."

Cora's smile faded. "Not a price. *Years*. Those are the years you had affairs with my husband."

The sisters again gasped in unison. Charlotte slapped her hand over her mouth to keep from yelping with surprise and delight.

"It was the Summer of Love," whined Penny.

"Yikes," said Charlotte. The image of Penny enjoying the Summer of Love curled her toes.

The others glanced at her, and she realized she'd spoken aloud. "Oh. Sorry. Go on."

Tabby thrust out two downturned palms and bobbed them up and down as if she was trying to calm a hysterical child. "Cora, *dear*, for my part, I have to say, it was the *eighties*. There were drugs. *So many drugs*. We didn't know what we were doing. And my husband had just died. I was in a strange place—and, Cora—you know your Bucky. When it came to women, he was always like a man fresh out of prison. He probably sneaked a twenty-three-year-old waitress into his own coffin."

Charlotte recoiled, stunned that Tabby would offer such a blunt assessment of Bucky's moral fiber.

Strangely, Cora's anger didn't double. Instead, she offered them a sweet smile.

"Yes. I knew Bucky. But it's too late to make *him* pay, isn't it?"

She slammed the door, and they heard it latch.

"But what do you want us to do?" whined Penny.

"You figure it out," trilled Cora from inside.

CHAPTER FOUR

Charlotte swirled her legs in the turquoise water of Declan's lap pool. She'd no sooner sat down with him to enjoy a glass of wine and watch the sky fade from cerulean to dusky orange than they heard his front door slam.

Seamus had returned.

Naturally, the everlasting houseguest that was Declan's Irish uncle appeared the moment they'd tried to steal an intimate moment together. Seamus had moved back to Charity from Miami the previous summer. Declan had offered him a temporary place to stay, but as Thanksgiving approached, it seemed less likely than ever that Seamus had any intention of moving out.

Seamus' manifestation was less annoying to Charlotte this time, though. She'd been about to convey the story of her afternoon with Penny, and he was saving her the need to repeat it.

"What are you two up to?" asked Seamus, sliding open the glass door that lead from Declan's living room to the lap pool outside.

"Speak of the devil," said Declan.

Seamus cracked his beer. "Why do people always say that when I enter a room?"

"I, for one, am glad you're here for once," said Charlotte.

"Thank you. I think."

Charlotte launched into the tale of meeting Cora and her strange interaction with Penny and her twin.

"You're kidding. I can't believe Penny has a twin. And they *both* slept with Cora's husband?" said Declan when she'd finished.

Charlotte nodded, still cackling at the memory of the twins' faces. "It sounds like Bucky was quite the Lothario. And I suspect Cora knew a lot more about his shenanigans than he thought she did. You should have seen her face. She's been *waiting* for the day she'd have the sisters over a barrel, frothing for that property."

"Has anyone asked where Cora was when Bucky took his swan dive onto the mast?" asked Seamus, slipping off his loafers. His toenails looked as if he'd spent most of the day hanging from a cave ceiling.

Declan winced. "Do *not* put those feet in my pool."

Seamus glanced down. "Oh. Sorry. I've been meaning to ask Jackie to cut those for me."

"But her chainsaw is on the fritz?" quipped Charlotte.

"Ha ha." Seamus plunged his feet into the pool, his tongue jutting at Declan.

Declan sighed and returned his attention to Charlotte. "So what's Penny going to do?"

"That's the best part. Penny wants me to help her figure out what will win over Cora."

"How are you supposed to do that?"

She shrugged. "I told her I was a detective, not a miracle worker, but she kept screaming *just keep track of your hours* at me, and that's hard to resist."

"This job will put you over the hours you need to get your license, won't it?"

She nodded. To apply for a private detective license, she needed forty hours of internship. Darla's husband, Frank, the local Sheriff, and Declan's uncle Seamus, a private detective himself, had already helped her earn most of them.

She turned to Seamus. "But it also means I need you to be the official hire, so it counts as an internship for me."

"Ah. Consider it done. So we have to figure out what Cora wants and get her to sell to Penny?"

"Yep."

Seamus grunted. "I'm not sure I'm the guy to hire to figure out what women want."

"Oh, I almost forgot," said Declan rising. He jogged into the house and appeared a moment later with a box wrapped in a thin kitchen towel held tight with safety pins.

He thrust it at Charlotte.

"What's this?" she asked.

"It's an early birthday gift, but open it now. I don't want you to go one more day without it."

"Ooh. How intriguing."

"Extra points for the wrapping job," said Seamus.

"Thank you. I was out of paper."

Charlotte undid the safety pins and unfolded the towel to reveal a square cardboard box, the graphics on which suggested there was a shiny *metal* box inside. She read the label.

"A video doorbell?"

"Yes. It will alert you when someone is at your door. Then you can see them and talk to them through your phone."

"But Mariska and Darla never bother to knock anyway. A door doesn't even slow them down. I can't imagine what a doorbell can do."

"It's not for them. You're doing all these dangerous things now, and you never know who might be lurking outside your door."

"Like Stephanie," muttered Charlotte, invoking the name of Declan's ex-girlfriend.

Declan sniffed. "I don't think she shows up on camera."

He pulled her close and kissed the top of her head.

Seamus rolled his eyes. "All right, that's enough of that."

CHAPTER FIVE

The Hock o' Bell Pawn Shop's bell rang as Declan entered, followed by what sounded like the moaning of a lonely banshee.

Wincing, his gaze settled on the source of the din.

A one-eyed cat.

The new employee, Blade, wore a pure white, one-eyed cat on his shoulder.

Sure. Why not.

Declan sighed, knowing this probably wouldn't even be the oddest thing about his day. With Blade, things only devolved.

Blade sat perched on a sofa not far from the door. He hadn't worked at the shop for long, and Declan felt that they might still be in the honeymoon phase. Already, using the word *odd* to describe him would be a disservice to odd people everywhere. Blade was one part strange, one part terrifying, and one part enigma. Six-foot-six of aging muscle, with a long graying ponytail and skin like a pair of leather boots, Blade stood unique among the people Declan had met to date. His teeth were as large and white as spotless dice, but for the two missing—one upper, one lower.

And his name was *Blade.*

Declan might have fired Blade from sheer terror, except that the geriatric colossus consistently charmed the shop's aging customer base into buying things—with actual money—that he'd been *begging* people to carry away for years. Because

Declan procured most of his inventory at estate sales in a town made up of seventy percent retirement communities, half his "customers" arrived to *sell.* The other half didn't have anything to do between water aerobics and the early bird special, so they strolled around the shop chattering about the things they recognized as once belonging to their less fortunate neighbors.

"Isn't that Josie's bird statue?"

"Oh, you're right. How awful."

"I always hated that thing."

"Me too."

"Wasn't that fond of her, either."

"Nope."

Somehow, big scary Blade made almost everyone who wandered into the shop totter back out with a ship wheel lamp, pewter alligator, or chipped teapot.

Everything that made Blade frightening to Declan enchanted the ladies of Charity, Florida. Sales increased, and that money paid for Blade's assistance and then some. Pre-Blade, Declan had worked eight hours a day, every day, and while he hadn't minded the schedule as a single man, now that he'd met Charlotte, he enjoyed his days off.

Declan dealt with Blade's idiosyncrasies—such as the one-eyed, howling cat draped over his shoulder like a burp pad—as they happened, never daring to anticipate the next.

"There's something different about you. I can't quite put my finger on it," said Declan.

Blade grimaced. "Aw, I'm sorry, man. I didn't have the *grooming* time I'd hoped to get this morning. Had to skip my hair products. I know you like me to look sharp when I'm here."

Declan's gaze swept over his employee's uniform for the day: jean cargo shorts and a t-shirt emblazoned with a heat-transfer image of crossed knives, each blade thick enough to give a grizzly bear pause.

It was possible the definition of *looking sharp* needed to be further clarified in the employee handbook.

Declan sucked his canine tooth with his tongue. Blade always wore his long, dishwater gray hair in a simple ponytail, so he was ninety-nine percent sure Blade was mocking his *own* grooming habits with that comment about using hair products.

He was also one hundred percent sure he wasn't going to do anything about it.

"I wasn't referring to your hair," said Declan, nodding his chin toward Blade's furry friend.

Blade patted the cat, who remained amazingly calm as the man's oven-mitt-sized hand lowered onto it. "Oh. You mean Spot. Yeah, that's a long story."

"Spot?"

Blade nodded.

"He's all white, isn't he?"

"Yup."

A silence fell, and Declan realized no further explanation would be forthcoming.

Don't ask. Don't do it. Don't break first—

"Why would you name an all-white cat *Spot*?"

Shoot. I asked.

Blade jumped as if he'd forgotten Declan was there. "Huh? Oh, I found him down at the bar I like to go to."

Silence fell once more, and Declan felt his fingers curl into frustrated fists and his voice notch up an octave.

"What's that got to do with naming him Spot?"

Blade blinked at him. "'Cuz that bar is my *spot*."

Declan exhaled.

Makes perfect sense.

He wasn't about to argue with a man whom he was pretty sure had worked as a mercenary at some point. The knife tee wasn't helping to dissuade him from that conclusion.

That tee.

I do have to say something about the dress code, though, don't I?

He'd only had an employee for a couple of weeks, and he already hated it. It turned out that being the boss wasn't any fun at all.

"So, Blade, about those knives on your shirt—"

Blade interrupted him. "Gerber silver tridents with double

serration, but I call them *Baby*—after the baby food—and *Stick*."

"*Stick*," echoed Declan. *After the action, no doubt.*

Hm.

The man named the knives on his *shirt*.

That's how much he liked knives.

Declan chewed at his lip and decided all was well.

Dress codes are such an antiquated idea, really.

He said the only word that came to mind.

"Neat."

Clearing his throat, he tried for a little levity. He surveyed the cat draped over Blade's shoulder and chuckled.

"With the one eye, he kind of looks like a pirate, but he's sitting more like a pirate's parrot."

Blade stared at him without comment.

Yeah. That was a stretch. Nevermind.

Defeated, Declan offered a quick nod and headed toward the back of the store. As he passed the sofa, he glanced back and noticed the cat's white legs hanging down Blade's broad back. It occurred to him *no* paws had hung down his chest.

He backed to his original position.

"Does Spot only have two legs?"

Blade nodded. "Now."

Silence filled the room, and a feeling of dread fell over Declan. He couldn't bear the idea of spending another twenty minutes dragging the story of the two-legged cat out of Blade. And yet—

The doorbell jangled, breaking the silence. Declan sighed with relief as two white-haired ladies entered the shop, wrapped in animated conversation. Spot again began to caterwaul.

Blade stood, and the ladies fell silent, their eyes following his ascent to its improbable height.

Declan watched them stare at each other.

Ah, the classic gunfighter stand-off between two little old ladies and a cat-clad giant.

The animal ceased its whining, releasing the women from their trance and launching them into coos of unrestrained affection.

"Look at that cat."

"Poor dear only has one eye."

Blade patted the animal and grinned with the enormous teeth he still possessed. "Yep. Lost a run-in with an alligator, I'm afraid."

"An alligator!" shrilled the ladies together.

"An alligator?" mumbled Declan. Though he still stood not far from Blade, it appeared his customers hadn't yet noticed him. He smiled and waved. "Morning, ladies."

The ladies ignored him and huddled around Blade as if he were a toasty fire on a winter's night.

Declan wandered to the counter where he thought he might be of some use.

Back on the floor, Blade continued his tale. "I found him close to dead on my doorstep and ran him to the vet. Nursed him back to health myself after the doctor did the hard stuff."

"Oh my, that was just wonderful of you," said one of the ladies, stepping closer.

Declan marveled at the scene playing before him. When the women looked at Blade, all they saw was an oversized teddy bear, not a tall-tale-telling, six-foot-six leather-man wearing elephant-gutting knives named *Baby* and *Stick*.

"Is he missing a leg, too?" piped the lady on the left.

Blade lifted the cat to offer his audience a better view. "Two. That's why he likes to pretend he's my parrot."

The ladies burst into giggles, and Declan's head snapped up from his paperwork.

That's my joke.

"My husband Charles would have loved that cat. He loved all cats, you know."

Blade gasped. "That's quite a coincidence. That's his name...Charlie."

The woman echoed his gasp. "No."

Declan watched the fibbing giant nod. "It is indeed."

The woman reached into her purse to retrieve a tissue as her eyes began to water.

Fifteen minutes later, the two women left, having purchased an ottoman, a wicker lounge chair, and a set of dishes Declan had been trying to unload for two years. The cat wailed until the door shut behind them.

"I thought his name was Spot?" asked Declan as he tagged the ottoman for delivery.

"Who?"

"*The cat.* You said you found him at the bar and named him Spot, but you told the ladies you found him on your doorstep, and his name is Charlie."

"Oh. I haven't settled on a permanent name. Charlie *is* a pretty good name. And you had a good point about him not having any spots and all."

Blade scratched the cat's ears until it rumbled like a Harley-Davidson, but its ecstasy was short-lived. Charlotte entered, and the cat broke into torturous song once more.

"Hey, Blade, I like your second head," said Charlotte over the wailing.

Blade stood, grinning ear to ear. "Well, thank you, Miss Charlotte. I found him outside my house, and he seems to like it up here."

Charlotte stretched to give the cat an ear scratch.
"Is it me, or does he not have any front paws?"

"Nope. Found him like this. Not sure if he was born this way or—"

"Or was nibbled by an alligator," grumbled Declan as he walked out to greet Charlotte, hoping he could steal the attention of his own girlfriend away from Blade.

He wasn't feeling confident.

"Hi," he said.

Charlotte's eyes remained on the cat as she winced. "Yikes. Poor thing."

"*Hello*," repeated Declan.

"Oh, hey," said Charlotte.

Declan sighed and turned to Blade. "So, can we settle on this much? You found the cat *post*-mangled. *Not* bleeding on your doorstep?"

Blade's expression turned coy. "Alligator attack makes a better story, though, don't it?"

"Sells more dishes, that's for sure."

Another customer entered, and the cat turned on his warning siren.

Charlotte frowned and pulled back her petting hand.

"It's not you. He does that every time someone comes in," said Declan.

She resumed petting. "I guess it's nice to have a shop greeter."

Declan grunted. He didn't really want a moaning cat to be the first thing the customers heard, but so far, it had only helped sales.

Blade wandered off to greet the customers.

Blade ended his shift with another stunning handful of sales, including a stuffed grouse Declan had regretted buying for months. When Blade lumbered home sporting his cat epaulet, Charlotte remained to talk through her latest case.

Although Declan loved discussing Charlotte's new career as a private detective, he found it unsettling that it sometimes brought her in contact with unsavory characters. At least they lived in Charity and not in a big city. And for the most part, her clientele needed help with missing lawn ornaments more often than missing bodies, but even so, he worried.

Sometimes he felt a little jealous. The most heart-pounding thing *he* did on a daily basis was stare holes through that stuffed grouse collecting dust on his shelf. The idea of never turning a profit on it had scared him to death, but it still wasn't quite the same.

As she chatted, his gaze wandered to a paycheck envelope on his desk. He picked it up. "Shoot. Blade left his check here."

Charlotte stood. "I have to go anyway. I can take it to him."

"You know where he lives?"

"I do. He chewed my ear off the other day when I came to see you and found only him. I know all about his place—the color of the walls, the sticky light switch in the kitchen—"

"I can't even get him to tell me where he found a cat, and he lends *you* his diary."

Charlotte put her hands on either side of her cheeks and posed. "I have a trusting face."

Declan squinted at her. "When he was here, and I wasn't, that was bad, right?"

"Bad? What do you mean?"

"I mean, you'd rather have found *me* here than Blade."

"Of course."

He smiled. "Good. Just checking. That devil is a *charmer*."

Charlotte laughed.

He handed her the check. "You can take it to him, but be careful. He could be an assassin."

"Oh, come on. He's a Teddy bear."

"Did you see his t-shirt? He told me his mother was a hippie and named him Blade after *grass*."

"Not true?"

"I don't know. But when he shows up wearing a shirt with enormous knives on it, I have to ask myself if he's being entirely honest."

She chuckled. "I'll be careful. You know me."

Declan sighed. "I do. That's what I'm afraid of."

CHAPTER SIX

As soon as Charlotte sat in the Volkswagen Bug she'd borrowed from Mariska, she could feel something was off. It took her a moment to identify the smell.

Chanel Coco Mademoiselle.

She'd smelled the perfume several times before but never in Mariska's car. Mariska's car smelled like baked goods and whatever tester perfume they had out at Costco that day.

Charlotte only knew one person who wore *Chanel Coco Mademoiselle.*

"Crouching on the floor of someone's car isn't the most lady-like move," she said, gaze trained on her rearview mirror.

A blonde head rose into view. Charlotte viewed it like a sunrise...rising on someone stranded in the desert.

Stephanie wiggled her fingers, waving to the mirror. "*Shoot.* I was going to pop up just before you drove away."

"*Shoot.*"

Stephanie Moriarty, Declan's ex-girlfriend, ran her fingers through her hair, raking the tussled mop back into place. She always possessed the look of a fresh-out-of-bed-yet-ready-for-a-night-on-the-town sex-kitten.

Charlotte hated that about her.

Stephanie had grown up in Charity with Declan. She was a lawyer and, more than likely, a psychopath.

"I have some news for you," said Stephanie.

"You could have come into the shop. Or—here's a novel idea—I have a *phone*."

Charlotte wanted to know how Stephanie had broken into her car but couldn't bear giving her the satisfaction of asking.

Stephanie dismissed her sarcasm with a wave of her blood-red, manicured nails. "Nah. I know you don't like it when I distract Declan."

Charlotte's fist curled at her side. "Funny. Now tell me what you want and get out of my car."

"It isn't what *I* want. It's what my client wants."

"And who's that?"

"Cora Bloom."

Charlotte turned to face Stephanie. "I thought you were a defense attorney."

"I'm a little bit of everything."

"Mm. Yes, that's true. I can think of a *few* things you are."

Stephanie smiled. "Cora has retained my services to handle details and assist her in deciding the winner of a competition between your client, Penny, and Tabby."

"Why do I have the feeling she didn't find you online?"

"She didn't. No, when I heard about this interesting turn of events, I offered my services."

"You mean when you heard Penny hired *me* to help her."

"What? Wow. Aren't you self-absorbed. The point is, there could be any number of things she'll require the eventual winner to accomplish, but there is one overriding theme worth the largest number of points—"

"You're judging us on a point scale?"

"—she wants you to find out who killed her husband."

Charlotte shifted to get a better view of Stephanie and to keep the frustration and awkwardness of their encounter from causing a crick in her neck. "What are you talking about? I thought Bucky fell?"

"We don't know that for sure."

Charlotte shook her head. "I'll pull out then. If I help Penny, you'll make sure she loses. I can't do that to her."

"If you pull out, she automatically loses."

"Who says?"

"I say."

Charlotte sighed. "Didn't the police already rule his death an accident?"

Stephanie smiled her snakiest grin and popped open the door. "Prove it then."

"Do you know something the police don't?" she called as Stephanie slammed the door.

If the blonde heard her, she offered no sign. Instead, she tip-toed off in her four-inch heels and slinked into her candy-apple red Dodge Viper before roaring away. She waved goodbye as she passed.

Charlotte squeezed the steering wheel until her fingers threatened to break. Stephanie wanted Declan back, but if she couldn't have him, she seemed content making their lives as difficult as possible.

Think, think, think.

Stephanie would load the deck against her. She'd try for maximum pain, all the while ensuring Penny *didn't* win, thanks to her association with Charlotte.

She had to stay two steps ahead of her.

Luckily, if one of the challenges was to find exactly *how* Bucky arrived at the wrong end of a sailboat mast, Penny already had the services of a detective. Well, one *almost*-detective plus Seamus, who was legit, if not a tad unorthodox and very annoying.

She needed to get to work *immediately*.

How had Stephanie found out about the competition so fast? Did she have connections to Cora? Or maybe Tabby?

Realizing she'd begun to sweat, Charlotte turned on the Volkswagen's air, retrieved her phone, and dialed.

"Hello?" said Seamus.

"Seamus, I'm glad I caught you. We have to find out how Bucky Bloom died."

"What? Who?"

Charlotte sighed. "I told you I needed you to take over Penny's case for me so I could use the internship hours, remember?"

"Right. Uh...remind me the facts again?"

"Penny wants Cora Bloom to sell her Cow Town, the pastures next to Pineapple Port. But Cora—"

"Oh, right, right—Penny has to compete against her sister. And the two of them both boinked Cora's shish-kebobbed husband."

"Right. At least you remembered the important parts."

"Always."

"Anyway, I just talked to Stephanie—"

"Ooh. I'm sorry I missed that."

"Uh huh. It was a joy, as always. I found her hiding in the back seat of Mariska's car, ready to leap out and scare me."

"Or slit your throat."

"Always a possibility. She discovered that I'm helping Penny and talked Cora into hiring *her* to plan and run the competition between the sisters."

"Then you should drop out."

"Tried. She said if I do, Penny automatically loses."

"Wow. So, she just wants to make sure you end up looking like an idiot."

Charlotte paused. "She wants to toy with me, no doubt. The point is we have to stay one step ahead of her. She all but told me the winner would be the one who solved Bucky's murder."

"I thought he took a tumble."

"I guess Cora thinks differently. Or she wants proof it was an accident."

"Okay. This is your operation. What do you want me to do, and, more importantly, when do I get my first check?"

"I have every intention of sharing the money—"

"I'm *kidding*. Sort of."

Charlotte laughed. "I'm going to see if Frank can dig up everything the cops know about Bucky's death. Maybe you can find out if Tabby hired someone to help her? It would be nice to see who we're up against."

"Smart. I'm on it."

"Thanks. Oh, one other thing. Stephanie found out about

this really fast. I know she keeps tabs on Declan and probably me, but it might be worth checking to see if she has connections to Tabby. I can't imagine Penny would have told her."

"Maybe Declan's house is bugged."

Charlotte's gasped. "You think? Is that possible?"

"We are talking about Stephanie."

"I know, but that's like *spy* stuff. How can we find out?"

"It's no problem. I'll get a bug detector and give the house a once-over. Leave it to me."

"*Thank you.*"

Charlotte hung up and took a deep breath as she imagined all the things she'd said to Declan in his home. She cringed, thinking Stephanie might have heard *everything*.

She took a moment to clear her mind and see the game from Stephanie's perspective. How had she been able to sweet-talk Cora into hiring her? Had Stephanie already turned Cora against Penny and her? Had Cora already made up her mind, thanks to Stephanie's meddling?

Wait.

How did she know Stephanie really met with Cora at all?

She dialed Penny.

"Penny, have you heard from Cora? Do you know anything about a lawyer working with her?"

"Yes, Cora called me fifteen minutes ago to tell me I'd hear from her lawyer. I figured she was trying to scare me, that vindictive b—"

Charlotte cut her short. "Hey, watch what you say. This is going to be more cutthroat that you know, believe me. You never know who's listening."

"What's that supposed to mean?"

"Just trust me and think only kind thoughts about Cora. Act like she's always in the room with you."

"Sounds like a nightmare."

"What did I just say?"

"Sorry."

"Did Cora mention her lawyer's name?"

"A Miss Moriarty? I recognized the name from that new

storefront out on the main drag."

Charlotte heard herself release the deep, guttural moan that sounded every time she heard Stephanie's name. "Yep, that's her."

"You heard from her? This lawyer?"

"Yes. She said the winner would probably be the one who solved Bucky's murder."

Penny gasped. "Bucky's murder? She thinks he was *murdered*?"

"I don't know. She might just want proof that he *wasn't*. It might be a lesson in futility created to frustrate us."

"Can you solve a murder?"

"If you remember, I have before. Declan's mother? The lady I found in my backyard?"

Penny grunted. "Mm. Right."

"Don't worry. I'm working with Declan's uncle Seamus. He's a licensed detective. We're already on it."

"Good."

"I'll let you know when I know more."

Charlotte disconnected.

So far, Stephanie was telling the truth.

That was a first, which worried her all the more.

Shifting into reverse, Charlotte noticed the paycheck envelope marked *Blade* on her passenger seat. She'd almost forgotten she had to deliver it.

She decided to call Darla's husband, Sheriff Frank, as soon as she'd run her errand to Blade's humble abode. Hopefully, he'd be open to gathering information about Bucky's murder for her. She needed all the help she could get.

CHAPTER SEVEN

Charlotte found a parking spot a block away and walked the short distance to Blade's house. Her path weaved closer to the curb as she passed the doll repair shop, Kewpie Kare, on the corner. She felt naked beneath the stares of a hundred miniature mannequins. The shop appeared closed, so she felt a little better knowing a locked door stood between her and the throngs of possibly possessed dolls.

What was the percentage of normal dolls to possessed dolls in the world? Eighty-twenty?

On Kewpie's door, someone had attached a note with an unnecessarily long piece of duct tape. The message had been scrawled with lipstick on half an envelope. She strolled past and then reversed, curiosity piqued.

Smelling the sweet, fruity scent of the lipstick, Charlotte figured someone had had to improvise after realizing they had no paper or a pen. Strangely, they *did* have a massive roll of duct tape.

She decided that wasting brain time solving The Mystery of the Lipstick Missive would have to wait for another day, but she did take the time to read the note.

"Joe, where are you?? Need Suzy!!" —Marg

Between the abundance of tape and exclamation points, Charlotte couldn't help but feel Marg had overcompensated for her lack of paper and pen. She was pretty angry about Suzy, too.

Eager to leave the doll shop's influence, Charlotte continued past a small convenience store called Quickie Stop and a side-by-side apartment before reaching the pink-painted cement block cottage Blade had described to her.

Imagine Pepto-Bismol was a house, he'd said.

He wasn't wrong.

She knocked, and Blade answered, his bulky frame filling the doorway.

"You forgot your check," she said, presenting the envelope.

"Oh, thank you, Miss Charlotte. I'd forget my head if it had been sawed off with a Buck knife."

Yikes. Declan's warning about Blade echoed in her mind.

Blade shifted to the left, revealing a sliver of the living room behind him. From what she could see, the room was empty but for a lounge chair and an olive-drab foot locker that appeared to be military issue.

A cat's head surfaced at one end of the chest, one remaining eye peering at her. She stared back as the head turned and floated along the edge of the chest before Blade's body blocked her ability to track it. The locker was much too tall for the cat to have been walking. She tried to work out how the face could have been floating—

Didn't that cat have a couple of missing legs?

"Hey, Blade—what can you tell me about that cat of yours?"

"You mean like where I found him?"

"That's a start."

Or if he's possessed by some kind of cat demon, perhaps the dolls were all filled-up...

Blade squinted at her. "You want the real truth? I like to tease Declan a little."

She chuckled. "The real truth."

He flicked a finger in the direction she had walked. "He was out there, in front of the convenience store, yowling at people as they went in and out. The owner tried to chase him away, but he kept coming back. I thought I better grab him before he ended up dead."

"How does a two-legged cat get chased away and come

back?"

Blade chuckled. "That's kind of a funny story—"

The cat's head bobbed behind the chest again, and Charlotte grimaced, unable to contain herself any longer. "I'm sorry. I don't mean to interrupt, and this is going to sound crazy, but I think I saw your cat's head floating behind your chest there."

Blade stepped to the side, and Charlotte yelped. The cat stood directly behind him, his head even with the big man's knee. Standing on his two remaining hind legs, the cat kept his balance by tottering back and forth like a tiny, furry dancer trapped in a constant state of cha-cha.

"He walks like a person."

"That was the funny story," said Blade, hoisting the cat and draping him over his shoulder.

"Did you decide whether you're going to call him Spot or Charlie?"

"Nah. I'm still thinking."

Charlotte chuckled. "Well, there's got to be a name for a cat that walks on two legs. Christopher Walkin'? Johnnie Walker Cat? Maybe *Boots*, because Boots is made for walkin'?"

Blade's eyes widened. "Ooh, I like Johnnie Walker."

"That's a good one. He looks like a Johnnie."

Blade nuzzled the cat, and, once again, Charlotte couldn't imagine Blade hurting a fly.

"Well, I better get going. See you later." She waved and took a few steps before turning back. "Hey, do you know anything about the shop on the corner?"

"The dolls?" Blade peered through his nearly closed door. "Nah. That place gives me the creeps."

CHAPTER EIGHT

Charlotte had been home in Pineapple Port for less than five minutes before Mariska and Darla knocked and entered, barely a heartbeat passing between each action. Charlotte watched her soft-coated Wheaten terrier, Abby, rub against the ladies in her typical, ferocious-guard-dog fashion.

Lull intruders into a sense of false security. That's her plan.

"What are you two up to?" Charlotte asked, unfazed by the familiar neighbor ambush.

"We were wondering if you wanted to go to *Apricot's* for dinner?" asked Mariska, invoking the name of a frequently visited hole-in-the-wall restaurant featuring the cheapest chicken-fried steak in town.

Charlotte's lip curled involuntarily. *Apricot's* food wasn't inedible, but the ambiance lacked something—for instance, a post-nineteen-eighty-two decor and plastic menus that didn't feel as if they'd served as the previous customer's *plate*. Wire clothing hangers dangled at every booth, serving as makeshift paper towel dispensers. She did appreciate those. They were a joy money couldn't buy.

"I'll pass, thanks."

"Your loss. Today's peach cobbler day."

Charlotte gasped. "Well, why didn't you say so?"

"So you'll go?"

"No."

Mariska huffed.

Darla finished petting Abby, much to Abby's chagrin, and straightened. "So what's new with you today, missy?"

"Oh, the usual. I have to solve a murder, and Declan's ex subtly reminded me that she'd love to murder me."

"Stephanie? What is she up to now?" asked Mariska.

"She's working for Cora Bloom, organizing this competition between Penny and Tabby."

"What were the chances of that?" mumbled Darla.

"I suspect it wasn't a coincidence. She hid in the back seat of the VW and then popped up to tell me I needed to investigate Bucky's death if I wanted Penny to win."

Mariska's eyes grew wide. "She hid in *my* car?"

Charlotte nodded.

Mariska scowled. "She better not have scratched it."

Darla patted Mariska on the arm and returned her attention to Charlotte. "I love coming over here. You always have the most interesting things to share. All I can report is what time my mail arrived and how long Frank was in the bathroom."

"Anything else?" prodded Mariska.

Charlotte shrugged. "Not about Penny's situation. Oh, Blade has a new friend."

"That's the man who works for Declan? The one with the summer teeth?" Darla pointed her index finger at her own mouth and swirled it.

Charlotte's brow knit. "Summer teeth?"

"Sum'r there and sum'r not?"

"Oh, ha. Yep. He found a cat with no front legs and was wearing it like a fur stole when I visited Declan."

Mariska put the tip of her fingers over her mouth. "Oh no, what happened to the poor thing?"

"Blade doesn't know. Found it that way. It also has one eye."

Darla snickered. "That's not a *cat*. That sounds more like a *ca—*"

Mariska's head tilted so far to the right Charlotte feared her neck had quit to join the circus. "What are you thinking?"

Mariska's lips drew into a knot. "This cat, does it walk on its hind legs?"

"Yes. How did you know that?"

"Mr. French over at the doll hospital had a two-legged cat that walked like a person. I guess they can all do that—"

"What color was his cat? White?"

"If I remember right. Why? Is this cat white?"

"Yes."

Mariska gasped. "So all cats with two legs are *white*?"

"*Noooo*, Blade lives two houses from the doll shop..."

"It's the same cat," said Darla, slapping the counter as if she'd just calculated Amelia Earhart's location.

"Did French's cat have one eye?" asked Charlotte.

Mariska shook her head. "I don't remember. I only saw it once driving Fay there to pick up the most darling little prairie-girl doll."

Darla snorted a laugh. "Fay loves her dolls. I think they're a substitute for that ungrateful daughter of hers."

Charlotte tapped her fingers on the counter, her memory wandering to the darkened Kewpie Kare. "The doll shop is closed, and there are notes on the door from people frantic for their dolls. No one can reach him, apparently."

"You don't think Mr. French would move and leave his cat behind, do you?" asked Mariska.

"He wouldn't have to walk away very fast," said Darla. Her voice was strained, a case of the giggles knocking at her door.

"You're terrible," said Mariska.

Charlotte did her best to ignore the situation, knowing full well she only had a minute or two before both Mariska and Darla were cackling too uncontrollably to be of any help. "Maybe I should grab Frank and swing by there to make sure something didn't happen to Mr. French?"

Darla nodded her approval. "I hope French didn't pay full price for that cat."

Mariska tittered. "Nah, it was half off."

The two women exploded with laughter, and Charlotte left

to find Frank. The ladies would be of no further help.

She spotted Frank tending to the small pond in his front yard. A ceramic frog sat on a stone beside him, holding a small rod and reel, forever fishing without bait.

"Get a new koi?" she asked, approaching.

"Nah. They're expensive little buggers. I'm just trying to keep the ones I have alive. They need more oxygen."

"I was wondering if I could interest you in checking out Mr. French's doll hospital."

Frank stood and wiped the sweat from his brow. "Kewpie Kare? What's up?"

"Blade, the guy who works for Declan, found French's cat, and there are notes on the door from people trying to retrieve their dolls."

"I think he lives over the top of the shop. It's probably the dolls that got him."

Charlotte chuckled. "That's my theory."

"Did Blade knock on the door and see if the man is missing a cat?"

"Blade doesn't know anything about the cat other than he found it. It was Mariska who knew Mr. French had a two-legged cat."

"Two?"

"Two. Walks on its hind legs like a person."

"You're pulling *my* leg."

"Nope."

Frank shrugged. "He's probably got a cold, but I'll check. It'll be worth it to see a walking cat."

CHAPTER NINE

Seamus eased to the guard box at the Silver Lake retirement community in his ancient Toyota. Parking Pass Pete stood inside the box, wearing his ill-fitting guard uniform. Pete lived in Pineapple Port but worked at rival Silver Lake, so whenever he was on duty, Charlotte and her cohorts had an in.

"Top o' the mornin' to you, Pete," said Seamus.

"It's almost dinner."

"Whatever. Hey. I need to meet with the head honcho. Can you tell me what house she lives in?"

Pete chuckled. "Tabby? She doesn't live in this place with the rabble anymore."

"No?"

"Nah. She has a big house on the other side of Silver Lake. All the better to peer down on the little people. Just bought it. Go around the community, and you'll see a dirt road with a big wooden dolphin for a mailbox. Can't miss it."

"Hm. Thanks. Take it easy."

Pete nodded once and opened the gate so Seamus could make a U-turn. Seamus waved as he passed and circled the community to the opposite side of the lake.

Following a small paved road, he crept along until he spotted a carved wooden dolphin mailbox fitting Pete's description. Pulling onto the dirt road beside it, he drove another five minutes before a large, new-built home loomed into view.

Seamus slowed his car to a stop.

A yellow, nineteen sixty-seven Mustang convertible sat in the driveway.

He'd seen one like it before.

It couldn't be.

A woman wearing a flowing, flowered jumpsuit exited the house, followed by a suave tan man with dark, slicked-back hair.

Edmundo Baron.

Edmundo "Fast Eddie" Baron had been Seamus' chief rival in the Miami investigative world. He'd always solved the largest cases and had his name splashed across the local papers. Nearly every client Seamus received came via Eddie's reject pile.

What is he doing here?

The woman with him looked like Penny, so he suspected he had the right house.

Seamus stepped out of his car. "Eddie."

The man smiled. "Seamus, my Irish friend. It's so good to see you." He opened his arms wide and slapped them around Seamus' shoulders, squeezing tightly.

Once released from the boa constrictor's grasp, Seamus cleared his throat and did his best to smile.

"What brings you to my neck of the woods, Eddie?"

Eddie glanced at Tabby and smiled. "Oh, you know. Business as usual. Seems they have to import talent in this neck of the woods."

Tabby held out her hand. "Tabby Trahan. And you are?"

Seamus tore his glare from Eddie. "Apologies. Seamus Bingham, nice to meet you."

"What brings you to my door, Mr. Bingham?"

Eddie slapped a hand on Seamus' arm and grinned. "Let me guess. You were hoping to get Ms. Trahan to hire you? But once again, I have beaten you to the punch?"

"No. I—" Seamus realized he didn't have a straight answer prepared. His plan had been to meet Tabby and poke around to see if she'd reveal what she knew and who she might hire. His plans had not included jockeying with his arch-nemesis.

Charlotte had only heard about the need to solve Bucky's death less than a day ago. Clearly, Tabby had known for much longer if she'd had time to call Edmundo from Miami. And if that was true—Eddie was no coincidence. Someone had done their homework. They knew Seamus would be working for the competition.

"They" had to be Stephanie.

Time for that later. Right now, he had to invent an excuse for being there. "I'm working for Penny. I thought I'd swing by and find out who Tabby hired. See if maybe we could all work together on this."

Eddie and Tabby burst into laughter.

"Why would we help *you*?" asked Tabby.

Seamus opened his mouth but failed to find an answer that wouldn't elicit further joy from Eddie.

"He's always been funny," said Eddie, slapping him on the shoulder as he headed for his Mustang.

Seamus' fingers curled into fists.

"I will be in touch soon," Eddie called as he pulled from the driveway.

"Anything else?" asked Tabby, arching an eyebrow in Seamus' direction.

Seamus considered trying to reason with Tabby and warning her about Stephanie's inclination for mischief.

Nah.

Let her find out on her own.

"No, I think that's all. Nice to meet you," he said, with a bow of his head. He turned and entered his own less-impressive vehicle.

Pulling back onto the dirt drive, he hit the first pothole and heard Tabby's voice behind him.

"Tell Penny she can go to—"

He turned up the radio and kept driving.

CHAPTER TEN

Charlotte and Declan liked to meet at his house in order to avoid the prying eyes of Pineapple Port. Retirees had a lot of free time to fill, and being nosy killed time.

At Declan's home, they had the opposite problem. Seamus didn't gossip and couldn't care less about their love lives. But he was *so* oblivious that it didn't occur to him that his almost constant presence—sitting in the middle of the sofa drinking a beer and watching Jeopardy—made romance difficult.

Seamus' hours were spotty at best. Sometimes he stayed with his girlfriend, Jackie, in Pineapple Port. Other times he stayed at Declan's, parked in front of the television like a piece of furniture or sprawled on almost any surface with a book in his hand, for days at a stretch.

The one thing he never seemed to do was find a house of his own.

Charlotte knocked, and Declan answered, throwing his arms open wide.

"Hello darling, I'm so glad you're here."

She cocked an eyebrow. "Huh?"

Declan placed his finger over his lips, asking her to be silent, and then poked his thumb in the direction of the living room. Charlotte tilted her head to peer past him and spotted Seamus inside, waving a black box over the coffee table. He glanced up and waved before holding his finger to his lips, requesting silence.

"I wanted to show you my new flowers out front." Declan walked past her, shutting the door behind him.

"He's sweeping for bugs?" she asked.

He scowled. "Yes. You might have told me you thought the place was bugged."

"Seamus suggested it was a possibility after I talked to you at the shop. You know, about the time Stephanie popped from my back seat."

"Seamus told me about that. You'd better start locking your car."

"That's the thing; I think I *did*. I don't know how she got in there. And keep in mind, if there *is* a bug, that means she was in your house, too."

The door opened, and Seamus joined them on the front porch.

"Living room, bedroom, and out back."

"That's where you found bugs? You're kidding," said Declan, eyes bulging.

"Bedroom?" mumbled Charlotte, the blood draining from her face.

Declan put his hand on his forehead. "Did you remove them?"

"Nope."

"No? Why not?"

"We might be able to use them to feed her bad information."

"Are we sure it's *her*?" asked Charlotte.

The men shot her withering glances.

"Okay. Dumb question."

Declan shook his head. "How am I supposed to live in a house knowing Stephanie can hear everything I do and say?"

Seamus shrugged. "For one, we can start eating out more often. Do you have your wallet?"

"Yes, but—"

"Great. I'll drive."

Seamus headed for his car.

"I'll drive," Declan called after him.

"Nope. My treat."

Declan sighed, and Charlotte led the way toward Seamus' clunker. She waved Declan to the passenger side and slid into the back seat. The leather had been rubbed paper thin by the passengers of countless previous owners. As she sat, stuffing poofed from the cracks like little geysers.

Seamus told them about seeing his nemesis, Edmundo, with Tabby.

Charlotte's phone rang its assigned jingle for an unidentified number. Shifting to reach for her phone pushed her tender flesh into a sharp spring hidden in Seamus' back seat. Her greeting sounded half *hello* and half yelp.

"You lost," said a familiar female voice.

"Stephanie?"

"Speak of the devil," yelled Seamus.

Charlotte motioned to him to be quiet.

"Darling Seamus. Did he like his present?" asked Stephanie.

Charlotte pulled the phone from her ear. "She wants to know if you liked your present."

Seamus looked in his rearview to meet eyes with Charlotte. "My present?" He made a noise as if he'd been lightly punched in the stomach. "She means Edmundo. It *was* her."

Charlotte raised her phone again. "Do you mean Edmundo?"

"Of course."

"Yep," said Charlotte, relaying the message to Seamus. Even seeing only a portion of his face, she could tell he was livid. She could feel her own ire growing to dangerous levels and tilted the phone closer to her mouth to be sure Stephanie could hear her.

"Did you ever consider getting a hobby, or, you know, a *life*, and maybe stop worrying about ours?"

Stephanie chuckled. "Playing with your lives *is* my hobby."

"You are a sad little person."

"Mm-hm. You're the one who should be sad. You lost because your client doesn't trust you. Seems your career is off to a roaring start."

"What are you talking about? Are you saying Penny lost?"

"Not the whole competition, but the first test."

"What first test?"

"See? Your client didn't tell you. I suspected as much. She didn't think she needed your help, apparently. That's got to hurt."

"You're such a—"

Stephanie had hung up, and Charlotte roared with frustration.

"What is it?" asked Declan.

"She called to tell me Penny had already lost the first test. I have to call Penny and find out what happened."

Jaw clenched, Charlotte dialed.

"Hello?"

"Penny, it's Charlotte. Do you know anything about a test from Cora?"

"It's taken care of," said Penny, her voice wrapped in a warm cloak of *smug*.

"What's taken care of?"

"Cora sent word that she'd had to let go of her gardener and needed a replacement. I sent the best landscaper in Florida, *The Art of Palm*."

"*The Art of Palm*? That doesn't even make any sense."

"Well, they cost a *fortune*. She's going to love them."

Charlotte chewed on her lip, running through all the reasons, besides the stupid name, that hiring *Art of Palm* had been a bad idea. It didn't take long.

"Oh no." Charlotte hung her head.

"What do you mean, *oh no*," asked Penny.

"I'll call you back."

"Do a U-turn," she demanded.

"What? But I'm starving—"

"Just do it. Please? We're not far. Run by Cora Bloom's house. I have to check on something for *our* case."

"Fine. You're buying appetizers now, though."

Seamus did a U-turn and headed for Cora's house. When

they arrived, Charlotte saw what she feared she would—Tabby on her hands and knees pulling weeds.

"Penny threw money at the problem instead of humility."

"What are you talking about?" asked Declan.

"Cora sent word that she needed landscaping, and Penny sent a company to do it. Tabby showed up in gloves, ready to get to work. That showed true penance. We lost the first test."

Edmundo came around the corner of the house, pushing a wheelbarrow. He spotted Seamus' car and waved, flashing his million-watt smile.

Seamus smacked his steering wheel. "Shite."

Tabby saw Edmundo waving and followed his gaze.

"Cora sent the landscapers away," she shouted in a sunny voice, her face covered in sweat and dirt. "I win!"

Seamus slammed the car into drive and headed back towards the restaurant, stewing in silence.

Charlotte redialed Penny.

"It's official. You lost that one."

"What one?"

"The gardening test."

"I sent her the absolute best. How is that possible?"

"Cora doesn't want you to *send* someone. She wants you to be *sorry*, remember?"

"I am sorry. I told you—they're incredibly expensive."

"You're not getting it. Sorry would be doing it yourself. Showing humility."

"Doing it—" Charlotte could hear Penny on the other end of the line sputtering with incredulity. "She wanted *me* to pick weeds?"

"Your sister is over there right now pulling weeds."

"Tabby? You've got to be kidding. I'd pay money to see that."

"You don't need to. Just drive to Cora's right now."

"She's a black hole of self-absorption. How did she figure it out?"

"Maybe she consulted with her investigator."

"You're saying *you* would have seen the trick?"

"It isn't so much a trick as a hope you'd make the more heartfelt choice, but yes, I would have been *looking* for the trick. We have to assume anything Stephanie asks us to do has a twist to it. You lost what will probably be the easiest test, and we don't even know how many tests there will be."

"You think I lost the whole thing already?"

"I hope not. But from now on, we have to be careful, and you have to tell me *everything*."

Penny sighed. "Fine. Sorry."

Charlotte was about to hang up when she heard Penny gasp.

"Are you okay?"

"I don't know. Do you think the landscapers will charge me, even if they weren't allowed to work?"

Charlotte sighed. "Goodbye, Penny."

CHAPTER ELEVEN

Three Months Previously

Stephanie glanced up from the contract she was reviewing and rubbed her eyes.

Why did I become a lawyer again?

She was trying very hard to settle down and act like a *normal* person, but it wasn't easy. It turned out that ordinary people spent an inordinate amount of time doing ordinary things.

Who knew?

The phone rang, and Stephanie answered, affecting a British accent.

"Stephanie Moriarty Law, how can I help you?"

There was a pause.

"Hello?"

"Does *anyone* fall for that?"

Stephanie closed her eyes.

"Hello, Mother."

"Hello, darling. How's my little chip off the old block?"

Normally, a mother calling a daughter was a heartwarming proposition. Less so when the mother was one of the most prolific serial killers alive. Stephanie had only been reunited with her mother, Jamie, recently. To say things weren't going smoothly would be an understatement, but the connection between them was undeniable, as much as Stephanie hated to admit it.

"Mother, why would you call me on the *phone*?"

"Because there was a line at the telegram office?"

"I mean, you're a *wanted woman*. For all you know, my phone is tapped." As she said it, Stephanie grabbed a pen and jotted *check tap* on the corner of a sheet of legal paper. If nothing else, her mother's call served as a nice reminder to cover the basics and give her office a good sweep.

"I just wanted to hear your voice."

"Right. For the second time in twenty-six years, you wanted to hear my voice. Really? *Stop*. I'm tearing up here."

"That's not fair."

"You gave me to *a stranger* at birth, Mom. How did you know she wouldn't turn around and sell me on the black market for fifty dollars and a bag of crack?"

"Do people sell *bags* of crack? Wouldn't it be a rock of crack?"

"I'm sure they put several rocks in a bag..."

"Hm. Would a baby cost a whole bag? Or—"

"Why are we talking about crack?" asked Stephanie.

"Sorry. Look, sweetheart, people didn't do things like sell babies for bags of crack rocks back then. It was a lot harder to sell a baby before Craigslist. I'm not even sure *crack* was a thing then—"

"That's really not the point. And don't call me *sweetheart*."

Jamie sighed. "I told you. I kept tabs on you. I was always watching. Do we have to do this every time I talk to you?"

"Maybe a few more times. I want to make sure I don't forget."

"Fine. Are we done now, for today at least?"

Stephanie sighed. "Yes. Fine. So tell me the real reason for your call if it isn't illegal."

"It's not. I need you to buy some land for me. A big empty field, to be precise."

Stephanie scowled. "Please tell me you're not moving back to town."

"No. I want you to buy a *specific* lot that I understand might be for sale now."

"Why?"

"Let's say I may have left some *loose ends* there from earlier in my career."

Stephanie lowered her head to her desk with a thud. "You're kidding me. Please tell me you're not saying what I think you're saying."

"I figure it would be better to buy the land and, uh, redecorate at my leisure before someone tries to dig a basement and finds uh—"

"Don't say it."

"You get it then."

"Yes, I'm not an idiot. Anyone listening to this call could figure it out."

"Oh, well then, bodies. There are bodies—"

"LA LA LA," Stephanie sang over her mother's voice. "I didn't hear what you said. Nor do I want to."

"Fine. But I need you to buy the lot."

"Of course. Should I just put it on my credit card? Unfortunately, I don't have any babies to trade for it."

"Negotiate the price, and I'll send you the money."

Stephanie rapped her knuckles against her head, her lips pressed together like a vice. She could feel a tension headache crawling up the back of her neck like a hundred-pound spider. Her own misdeeds rarely caused her a moment's regret, but every word from her mother's mouth sent her into a panic attack. "Give me one good reason I should do this for you."

"I'm your mother?"

"You'll have to do a lot better than that."

"Let's just say it would behoove you to do as your mother asks. On a multitude of levels."

"Is that a threat?"

Jamie laughed. "It would be a last resort. I have plenty of options. For instance, after you revealed yourself to me, I did a little digging. I know a love story about a patch of swamp land in Argentina and a young man named Emile. Didn't you introduce those two? Has anyone seen Emile lately? I mean, since—"

"Enough," said Stephanie. The last thing she needed was her mother babbling about her own indiscretions on the phone.

If the Cheshire cat smiling had a sound, Stephanie was listening to it on the other end of the line.

"Write this down," said Jamie.

Stephanie grabbed a pen and transcribed her mother's instructions and a name. *Bucky Bloom.*

Jamie wanted to buy the enormous lot behind Pineapple Port—the one people called Cow Town—the most desirable piece of land in the whole miserable city.

She recognized the owner's name, too. Bucky Bloom had once owned all the land on which Charity now sat. He wasn't a man who needed money. He'd been sitting on Cow Town for decades.

"What if he doesn't want to sell?" she asked.

"He won't. But you'll find a way to make it happen. I have faith in you."

Stephanie flopped back in her chair. "Well, it's been a pleasure, Mom. By all means, please keep in touch."

"Oh, I will."

Stephanie disconnected.

What a nightmare.

In a fit of pique, she stabbed her pen into her leather desk blotter several times and then flopped forward on her desk.

Calm down. Think.

Stick to the basics, and you'll be fine—blackmail, sex, and threats.

Stephanie retrieved her phone and dialed the one person she knew who could help.

Her hair dresser, Raelyn.

Raelyn had attended high school with Stephanie and had *always* been a one-stop shop for gossip. Becoming a hairdresser had been less of a vocation and more of a *calling* for her.

The salon's receptionist answered, and upon request, Stephanie heard her holler for Raelyn. She sounded as if she'd won a hog-calling competition at some point in her life.

"Hello?"

"Hey, Raelyn. It's Stephanie."

"Well, heeeeeey. How you doin' Stephie?"

Raelyn's voice shifted into a happy, sing-songy gear. Upon reconnecting, Raelyn had been visibly impressed by Stephanie's expensive clothes and sophisticated manner. Stephanie suspected Raelyn thought that, with enough time, she'd find a way to con her old-new fancy friend out of money or favors.

It was adorable.

Stephanie had chosen Raelyn to do her hair intentionally, and it had nothing to do with her prowess with a pair of shears. She only ever had the dead ends snipped off; a Labradoodle could be trained to trim her hair.

But a high-priced mutt could never be the treasure trove of information that was Raelyn.

"I'm just fine, Raelyn. Thank you for asking."

"You need a trim? Going to take me up on that little poof of perm?"

"Uh, no. You know, I'd *love* to come in, but right now, I just have a silly question for you. Someone was in my office here a moment ago, and they mentioned Bucky Bloom. That name sounded so *familiar*, but I couldn't place it. I thought to myself, *you know who would know? Raelyn.* Was he on the football team or something?"

Raelyn laughed a low, harsh laugh that morphed into a coughing fit.

"You silly, Bucky Bloom's the rich guy. The dude who used to own all the land around here."

"Oh yeah? That sounds familiar—"

"Of course it does. He lives in that giant house out there by Cow Town—oh, and Stephanie... You would not believe—"

Here it comes. The meaty stuff.

"—that man is such a *dog*. He thinks if he throws money at a girl, she'll crawl right into bed with him."

"You don't say? Where did you hear this?"

She laughed again. "Didn't you ever wonder where I got the

money for that sweet Camaro the year we graduated?"

Sure. Keeps me up at night.

"You didn't."

"I did. The price was right for a little attention." Her voice dropped to a raspy whisper. "But don't you tell Paul I said that."

Paul was her husband. They'd known each other since middle school.

"No, of course not, Raelyn. It's all coming back now. Wasn't Bucky into some other dirty things?"

There was silence but for a faint jingly noise. Stephanie guessed Raelyn was shaking her head, and her trademark oversized earrings were chiming.

"No, no. Not that I can think of. He's just a *dog*. Lays low other than that. Never see him unless he's out sniffin' for women less than half his age."

"Hm. How about that. Thank you, Raelyn, that was driving me crazy."

"Sweetie, I totally understand. The other day I got to trying to remember the name of the band that sang that song that goes pum pum, pum pumpity—"

"Oh. Sorry Raelyn, that's my other line. I gotta go, but I'll see you soon."

Raelyn was still speaking as she disconnected.

So Bucky has a thing for the ladies.

Stephanie nodded.

That was a foible with which she could work.

CHAPTER TWELVE

The next morning, Charlotte heard a knock on her door as she was piecing together the video doorbell Declan had given her. Her gaze swept to her blinds as Abby-dog bounded to the door barking her deep-chested *woof*.

The blinds were open. She'd feared she'd forgotten to open them and accidentally alerted the Death Squad—a group of morning walkers who liked to confirm all the Pineapple Port residents had survived the evening. Early morning knocks were usually that morbid pack, checking to see if she'd had a stroke overnight. She'd tried to convince them that, as she was the youngest community resident by almost thirty years, maybe it wasn't necessary to check on *her*, but to no avail. In the end, she decided to sit back and accept their attention as a compliment. They didn't check if *everyone* was alive.

She peered out the window and found Sheriff Frank on her doorstep.

"You're out early," she said, opening the door. Abby piled out and slammed into Frank's knees before commencing her *I-know-you* happy dance.

Frank scowled. "What time do you think I go to work in the morning? I can't sleep all day like some of the layabouts in this place."

"Sorry. I guess I meant you're usually at work, so I don't see you until later in the day. As a rule."

"That's more like it. Anyway, I thought maybe we could have a cup of coffee and look at a dead body if that works for you?"

"Sounds delightful. Anyone I know?" She stepped back to allow Frank through the door, and Abby followed behind like a cream-colored shadow.

He held up a manila envelope. "Got the report back on Bucky."

"Ah, great." She poured a cup of coffee and handed it to him as he sat at the table. Luckily, she hadn't had her own cup yet, because, after years of practice, she'd finally learned how to make about a mug and a half of coffee using *just* the right amount of beans. Mariska, the neighborhood's biggest coffee snob, had ruined her for using pre-ground coffee.

She hadn't been expecting a guest, so she poured herself what was left and pretended her mug was full.

Frank pulled a blue file folder from the envelope, spreading papers across her table top.

A photo of a purplish, naked man lying on a slab caught her eye.

Frank grimaced and moved papers to cover Bucky's naughtier bits. "I'm going to be cremated. I don't want anyone taking naked photos of *me*."

"You should try harder not to be murdered then. This was an autopsy. He didn't have a whole lot of say in the matter."

"Does that mean I have to be nicer to people?"

"It wouldn't hurt."

Frank grunted.

"Did they say anything when they gave you this stuff?" asked Charlotte, skimming the medical examiner's report.

"Said there wasn't anything that screamed murder. Turns out he was pretty drunk at the time. The only thing out of place was some odd bruising."

"This?" Charlotte asked, pointing to a circular bruise on Bucky's upper chest.

He nodded. "But who knows exactly how he fell or what he hit on the way down."

"Other than his mast."

"Other than that. *That*, we're pretty sure about."

"So you don't think it's murder?"

Frank shrugged. "Nothing to say it is. Nothing to say it isn't."

"Do you mind if I keep this stuff for a while? I might go through it a little more closely later in the day when my stomach is stronger."

"It's all copies. Keep it."

Frank took another gulp of coffee and stood. "What are you doing today?"

"I thought maybe I'd go check out the scene of the impaling. See if anything rings a bell for me."

"You want to check on that doll hospital first?"

"Sure!" Charlotte heard the excitement in her own voice and felt a little ashamed. "Sorry. I shouldn't be so nosey. It's probably nothing, but I figured it wouldn't hurt to make sure Mr. French is okay."

Frank nodded. "Nah, it's a good instinct. Him being gone and his cat roaming the streets. It's odd."

Charlotte gathered a few things and tucked her hair into a ball cap. She slipped her lock-picking case into the waistband of her shorts and, noting that her tee didn't hide the bulge of the pack, changed into a larger, flouncier shirt. Frank didn't approve when she fudged the law but sometimes fudge made life much sweeter.

She said goodbye to Abby and headed for Frank's patrol car.

Ten minutes later, the two of them stood peering into Mr. French's store. Glass eyes stared back at them from every shelf. The hand of a large, brunette doll in a Victorian collared dress appeared to move ever so slightly, and Charlotte stepped back.

Trick of the light.

Right?

She shivered. "You say he lives over the shop? You couldn't *pay* me enough."

Frank flicked the lipstick message as if noting that it hadn't been removed and tried the door. "It's locked."

"I'll go around the back." Charlotte jogged away before Frank could stop her. She knew Frank wasn't allowed to enter a locked property without good cause but, well, *technically,* she wasn't allowed to either.

Still, what he didn't know wouldn't hurt him.

Charlotte tried the back door and found it locked as well. None of the windows wanted to budge. Pulling her black lock-picking case from her waistband, she removed the tools and got to work.

It was Frank's own wife, Darla, who'd taught her how to use the lock picks. Before she'd met Frank, Darla had a brief affair with the *other* side of the law.

Charlotte *loved* that Darla had shared her skills. People often considered retirees weak, less fashionable shadows of their younger counterparts. But she knew the truth. Retirement communities were full of long, rich lives filled with secrets most youngsters couldn't begin to imagine.

The door lock opened with a satisfying *pop!* Charlotte tucked away her tools and entered.

She felt like she'd arrived at the set of a zombie movie. Doll heads, legs, arms, eyes, and torsos littered every counter top. She avoided looking at them and weaved her way to the front of the store.

Don't think about tiny hands grabbing your ankles. Do not.

She opened the front door, heart racing, never so happy to see Frank's grumpy puss.

"The back door was open," she said, flashing doe-eyes and a smile.

He frowned. "Uh huh. You forget I've *seen* you and Darla working those locks."

"I'm sure I don't know what you mean."

Frank stepped inside and flipped the light switch. "Did you see anything?"

"I was trying really hard not to look. The workshop's like Dollmageddon. I feel better now that you're here."

They moved from room to room, finding nothing of interest other than a photo on the bedroom dresser of a mustachioed man Charlotte assumed was Mr. French. He had Blade's new cat draped over his shoulder. There was no mistaking it was the same cat.

They made their way back to the front, and Frank opened the door to leave. "I can try and reach his family—"

Frank cut short, peering down at a cat that stood on its hind legs, staring back up at him.

"That is the smallest, hairiest person I've ever seen."

Charlotte pointed. "See? I told you. That freaky thing is the perfect pet for this crazy place."

The cat tottered around them, appearing to search the lower level for his missing owner. With great leaps, he tackled the stairs toward the apartment above.

"This is breaking my heart," said Charlotte. She scooped up the cat and carted him around the small upstairs apartment, allowing him to inspect every inch. Feeling as if they'd looked everywhere, she sat him on the bed to be sure he was satisfied.

The cat rolled back on its haunches, looking very *un*satisfied.

"Oh, kitty. I don't know where he is. We'll find him."

Charlotte heard a bell outside, much like the one Declan had on his shop door. She glanced at the cracked bedroom window, and the cat took the opportunity to dive off the bed and half-walk, half-roll down the stairs.

"Hey!"

Charlotte ran after the cat and, arriving on the lower level, grabbed Frank's arm.

"Where'd he go?"

Frank stood in the entrance, staring down the street.

"He just rolled past me like a little mall walker."

"And you let him go?"

"He didn't go far. He's in front of the convenience store, wailing at the door."

As Frank said it, Charlotte heard the yowling. She passed Frank and walked to the cat as he fell silent. Picking him up, she entered the store.

A thin, youngish man stood behind the counter, ringing up

a customer. As she entered, the bell jingled, and the cat whined his discordant song. The man's attention shot to the cat, his expression twisting into an angry scowl.

"You can't come in here with that thing."

"Do you recognize him?"

"Who?"

"The *cat.*"

The man scoffed and handed his customer change. He made it clear he had no intention of looking at her again.

"Lady, I get enough crazy people in here. I don't need this."

"So you've never seen this cat before?"

Charlotte moved closer to the counter, and the cat hissed, eyes locked on the man. She could feel its back legs scrambling against her as if the cat wanted to launch himself at the cashier.

The man stepped back and pretended to straighten his shelves. "*I just hate cats.* You wouldn't bring a cat into a *Seven-Eleven,* and you can't bring them in *here.* Get out before I call the cops."

"No, please, let *me,*" she muttered, walking back to the entrance.

She spotted Frank on the other side of the glass, about to enter. Holding aloft her palm, she asked him to wait. Slowly, she eased open the door, careful not to shake the bell.

The cat remained silent, and Frank entered.

"Is there a reason we had to do that in slow motion?" he asked.

"Testing a theory. I think it's the bell that the cat doesn't like. This guy says he's never seen this cat before, but the cat sure seems to know him."

Frank approached the counter. "You work here?"

The man looked up, saw Frank's uniform, and snarled. "No. I just like to hang out behind the counter."

Frank glowered. "Maybe you didn't see the badge. I'm going to try this again. *Do you work here*?"

"Look, I not only work here, I *own* the place, and I'd really like to get back to work."

"What's your name, son?"

"Cody Sobeck."

"Do you know the guy next door? Mr. French?"

"The doll guy? We've said *hi.* We're not best friends or anything. Why?"

Frank pointed toward Charlotte, who remained at the entrance peering over the cat. "That's his cat. He's gone missing."

"The cat? He's right *there.*"

"*French* has gone missing."

"Oh. Right. Well, I'm sorry to hear that, but I don't know anything about it. Hope kitty finds a new home."

Frank hooked his thumbs into his belt. "Oh? Are you so sure he's not coming back to claim the cat?"

"Come on. Don't put words in my mouth, man. You know what I mean."

Frank craned his neck. "Mind if I look around?"

"What? Look, no offense, officer, but if you want to look around here, you get a warrant. I know my rights. I don't know anything about your cat or the freak next door."

Frank grunted. "Uh huh. I'll see you soon."

He motioned to Charlotte to follow him.

"Don't you think he's up to something?" she asked, scurrying outside behind him.

Frank sighed. "Maybe. But I *do* need to get a warrant to look around. And I have to hope an agitated cat is enough reason to get one."

"What are your chances of getting one?"

"Pretty good. I still have a little pull around here. But it will have to wait until Monday. I'm not going to use up a favor over a suspicious cat on a weekend."

Charlotte sneezed. She was allergic to cats and, as a rule, avoided touching them, but this one was trying to tell her something. She could feel it.

Blade padded down the street toward them, wearing a fuzzy brown robe snuggled around his large frame. "You found Johnnie." He lifted the cat and placed it on his shoulder. "Where'd you find him? I opened the door, and he shot right out."

"You couldn't catch a two-legged cat?" asked Frank.

"I was in my skivvies. I went to grab my robe, and he was gone."

"You know anything about this guy?" asked Frank, pointing to the man inside the convenience store.

Blade shrugged. "Just a guy. Not very friendly. Brags a lot about how he's going to get a Seven-Eleven franchise."

"In that dinky, dirty shop? I doubt it," muttered Charlotte.

Frank shrugged. "I'll check on him come Monday. Right now, I need to swing you back home and get to work."

"Sure," said Charlotte, her mind already whirring with an idea.

CHAPTER THIRTEEN

Back home, Charlotte spent two hours poring over Bucky's police report, beginning with her number one suspect, the person who was there when Bucky died. Shuffling through the paperwork, she found Bucky's mistress' name, *Shawna Taylor,* twenty-seven years old.

Twenty-seven?

Bucky was sixty-five.

Ew.

She jotted Shawna's name and phone number on a piece of paper, along with a few other notes. It seemed to her that the police had done a thorough job in the short amount of time they'd had. Maybe the whole case would boil down to exactly what it looked like, a terrible accident.

Telling Cora that her husband was *pretty drunk at the time* didn't feel like crack investigating, especially if Tabby's team proved foul play.

She searched for Shawna's name online and found her social media accounts. A relatively new picture of the girl with a young man caught her eye. Shawna and a man around her age had posed for a selfie beside a pile of clothes and what looked like athletic equipment. He wore a tee with FIU on the chest.

A quick search for FIU led Charlotte to Florida International University in Miami.

Moving in! was the caption on the photo.

Hm.

Was that Shawna's other boyfriend? Did he find out about Bucky and push him off the building in a fit of rage?

Something to keep in mind.

Finding nothing else suspicious in the police reports, she borrowed Mariska's car and headed for the marina where Bucky had taken his swan dive.

Sealock Marina was a large but quiet place. Apartments filled most of the building from which Bucky had tumbled. A few businesses occupied the lowest level.

She spotted a man exiting a real estate office and, posing as an interested buyer, asked him about the building. He shared that the apartments were mostly second homes and vacation properties, empty most of the week. The businesses on the lower level weren't the sort that drew much foot traffic. The marina itself came alive only on weekends.

His description of the area meant it was reasonable that no one saw Bucky's fall. It also made the marina the perfect spot to keep an apartment earmarked for marital extracurricular activity.

The police had interviewed Shawna and released her, but she was next on Charlotte's list. In a personal relationship with him and nearby when he died, Shawna might not have pushed Bucky, but she *had* to know something.

Charlotte took the elevator to the twentieth floor and searched until she found a sign that read *Roof Deck*, pointing to a stairwell. Yellow police tape that had once blocked the entrance to the roof had come loose and fallen to the ground.

It's not official if it's on the ground. She pushed on the door to head outside and found that the *roof deck* was a bit of a grandiose term for what greeted her. It was really just a roof with the usual array of blacktop, pebbles, and vent pipes.

Walking to the railing, she peered down at the boats below until she found the spot where Bucky must have been standing before he fell. Bucky's mast had been removed as part of body recovery, but his sailboat still bobbed in its oversized slip.

She wondered if boat salesmen had to reveal deaths to

potential buyers the way real estate agents had to by law. How would they even begin to explain where Bucky had died?

The railing that encircled the roof seemed low; a cement wall with metal working embedded in the top, supporting a stainless steel handrail. It came to her ribcage, so it wasn't out of the realm of possibility that a tall man like Bucky might have tumbled over. His blood alcohol level had been nearly point-one-five, and that, combined with any number of medications that an older man might be taking—anything was possible.

She jiggled the rail to see if it was loose. It held fast. She noticed remnants of dust where the police had searched for fingerprints. She dragged her hand along the handrail, strolling down the edge of the building, deep in thought. Ten feet from the spot she'd started, she noticed a black blob on the cement wall. Squatting to inspect it, she chalked it up as a bird dropping until a terrible stench triggered something in her memory.

Where do I know that smell?

She leaned her nose closer to the blob and then jerked away, regretting the decision.

I don't know what they're feeding the birds around here—

Oh no.

I hope it isn't Bucky.

She grimaced and took a few steps back. Shielding her eyes from the sun, she surveyed the area. The roof was like a vast empty plain, filled with nothing of interest to anyone but an air-conditioning repairman. She didn't know what she'd expected. It wasn't as if she thought she'd arrive to find a man wringing his hands like an old-time movie villain, cackling about how he'd pushed a man to his death. But she hated not finding *anything*. The case of Bucky's demise was rapidly spiraling toward a dead end.

She pirouetted in slow motion, searching for any sign of a camera that might catch a glimpse of the roof.

Nothing.

The marina apartment building stood taller than any of the others in the area, so without a drone or a satellite, it was unlikely any part of Bucky's time on the roof had ended up on film.

Time for Plan B.

Charlotte pulled her note sheet and phone from her pocket and dialed the number written there.

"Hello?" said a young woman's voice.

"Ms. Taylor?"

"Yes?"

"Hi. My name is Charlotte Morgan. I'm an investigator looking into Bucky Bloom's death."

Charlotte cringed, both because she wasn't *officially* an investigator and because she didn't know what effect uttering Bucky's name might have on Shawna. She might slam down the phone or scream or—

Shawna gasped. "Do you think something happened? What can I do?"

Or very pleasantly answer questions.

"No, I didn't mean to alarm you. I don't *think* something happened—"

"But you said you were an investigator?"

"I'm just glancing over the case, double-checking things."

Charlotte decided it would be unwise to mention any connection with Cora to Bucky's mistress. She suspected mistresses disliked hearing about wives almost as much as wives disliked hearing about mistresses.

"Do you mind if I ask you a few questions?"

"No. Any way I can help..."

"I know the police have already spoken with you, but it would help to confirm a few things. You were on the roof with Mr. Bloom the day he fell, correct?"

"Yes. But not when he fell. I was, like, *talking* to him, and he told me to go get ready for dinner, so that's what I did. When I came back, he was gone, and I heard people downstairs making weird noises, so I looked over the rail, and there he was."

Charlotte heard her suck in air as if trying not to cry. No matter how questionable Shawna's relationship with Bucky was, it had to be a shock to see someone you'd been talking to a moment before pinned to the end of a sailboat mast.

"And on your way back to the apartment, you didn't see anyone else heading for the roof? Or pass anyone else in the stairwell or the halls?"

"No. I told the police there was nobody. That place was like a ghost town during the week."

"Did you know anyone who wanted Bucky dead?"

There was a pause.

"Shawna?"

"What's that?"

"Did you know anyone who might have wanted to hurt Bucky?"

"Oh, no. He was a nice man. Maybe his wife?" She chuckled, but in a sad way, not with malicious joy.

Charlotte recalled the pictures she'd seen on Shawna's Instagram and decided she had to ask about the young man.

"Do you have a boyfriend?"

Shawna scoffed. "I did. He's dead, remember?"

"No, I mean someone *other* than Bucky."

"What? No. I loved Bucky. I know it seems crazy with him being so old, but he was *so* nice to me. I never had anyone take care of me the way he did."

Charlotte considered how to ask her next question and then plunged ahead. "As, uh, part of routine detective business, I, uh, *happened* to notice a young man in a picture with you on your Instagram. He's not your boyfriend?"

Charlotte winced. There were so many things wrong with her question. *Routine* detective business? What was that? And if it really was standard practice, how did it *happen* to happen?

I really need to work on my investigator-ese.

Shawna hemmed as if trying to imagine what Charlotte had seen. "A man in a picture? I mean, I have all kinds of pictures on my Instagram..."

"Sorry. It was you and a young man standing next to a pile of sports equipment? I think he had a college shirt on. FIU?"

Shawna laughed. "Oh. That's my brother, Dallas. He's staying with me because he needs to make more money to go back to college. What a joke. He'll never leave my house. He'll be sixty before I ever see my guest room again."

Charlotte chuckled. "I know someone like that. I feel for you."

So much for the jealous boyfriend theory.

"Hey, why did you ask me that? You don't think we had something to do with it, do you? Are the police looking into us?"

"No. Not at all. Like I said, standard investigatey stuff. Covering my bases."

"Okay. Because that would be messed up. I'm the only person who really loved him. He said his wife hadn't slept with him in, like, twenty years or something crazy."

Whoops. Too much information.

"Okay then. Don't worry, and thank you. You've been very helpful."

"Could you call me if you find or hear anything?"

"I will. I promise."

Charlotte disconnected and slipped her phone back into her pocket.

Still holding the sheet of paper in her hand, she stared at the railing.

Dead ends. I hate them.

She used the paper to scoop up the smelly goo she'd found on the wall, carefully folding the note into a little box shape she wished was airtight.

CHAPTER FOURTEEN

Charlotte made herself a liverwurst sandwich on rye and gobbled it down. Retirement-community-living influenced some of her life choices, and she knew her affinity for liverwurst was one of them. She never saw young people on television or in movies clamoring for liver paste and mustard. She even buttered the bread, like Mariska had done for her when she was a child.

She threw in some laundry and puttered around the house straightening.

What next.

Waiting for Stephanie and Cora's next challenge infuriated her, so she was left with nothing to do but work on determining if Bucky's death had been an accident or not. She still didn't feel like she had anything good to share with Cora. Nothing that would seal the win.

I need to jumpstart my brain.

She retrieved a piece of chalk from her kitchen utility drawer and stood in front of the wall she'd painted with chalkboard paint. It served as a catch-all for lists, doodling, and problem solving.

Rolling a piece of chalk in her palm, she stared at the blank, black wall.

Start somewhere.

She scrawled *Suspects* in large print, starting as high on the wall as she could reach. Bucky didn't seem like a stand-up guy, and the last thing you wanted to do was run out of space for suspects.

Her number one suspect remained Shawna, if only due to her proximity to Bucky at the time of his death.

She chalked it onto the board.

1. Shawna Taylor

She thought about the girl. The police report noted Shawna had been seen on the elevator camera heading down from the roof deck about the time she said she left Bucky to get dressed for dinner. She didn't appear again in the elevator, but she could have taken the stairs. There were no cameras in the stairwells.

Who else would want Bucky dead?

She stretched to add number two.

2. Cora Bloom

According to the cardinal *Dateline* rule, spouses were always top suspects. Bucky repeatedly cheated on her, giving Cora plenty of motives. It was hard to imagine little Cora jogging up the marina building stairs and shoving big Bucky over the edge, but she had to remain a suspect. She could have hired someone to do the dirty work.

With that thought, Charlotte edited Cora's entry on her board.

2. Cora (hired killer?)

She wondered if the police had checked Cora's bank account for unusual withdrawals. Probably not; they didn't consider Bucky's death a murder.

I need a hacker. A friendly hacker—not to do anything evil, just to take itty-bitty peeks at things.

She started a new list.

TO DO

1. Befriend a hacker.

Okay. Back to business.

Who else could have wanted Bucky dead? Deadly sins were always a great source of murderous intentions. She started with *envy-jealousy*:

3. Shawna - secret boyfriend?

Maybe Shawna had a boyfriend after all? She'd liked Shawna during their brief conversation. She had some daddy issues, dating a man forty years her senior, but she'd been nothing but polite and helpful on the phone. She didn't want to find the girl guilty, but that didn't mean she wasn't covering for a lover who didn't like sharing her with grandpa Bloom.

4. Bucky's other mistresses?

As a serial cheater, she knew that Bucky didn't restrict his extracurricular activities to Shawna. Perhaps previous mistresses didn't appreciate being replaced? Other women had to accept the existence of Cora, but they didn't have to tolerate the existence of Shawna. Maybe one of Bucky's mistresses decided if she couldn't have him to herself, no one could.

Charlotte tapped her fingernail on her teeth, trying to remember another deadly sin.

Ah. *Wrath* was always good for a murder or two.

5. Boyfriend/Husband of another mistress.

Who said Bucky was the only one cheating? If Shawna's imaginary boyfriend could work himself into a murderous rage, couldn't the boyfriend or husband of one of the other mistresses?

6. *Friend or business partner.*

Maybe a greedy partner stood to inherit a shared asset? Or his or her pride couldn't take Bucky's success?

Not every deadly sin fit. Lust wove itself into many of the other ideas on the list. Gluttony didn't work—no one killed Bucky because he stole the last piece of the pie. He did have a gluttonous appetite for other women, though, so that worked.

Sloth didn't work at all. Indolent people didn't work up the urge to murder people. Murder was a lot of work.

Unless Bucky was too lazy to walk down the stairs and took the shortcut over the rail instead...

She giggled to herself and then sobered.

That's terrible. Stop that.

She stared at her list. She didn't know enough about Bucky's personal life to know if any of her other ideas might be true.

The competition would be over before she had the time to trace all possible leads. She couldn't count on solving Bucky's death. She had to be ready to win the next competition.

She was about to walk away from the board when she felt compelled to back up and add one more possibility to the list.

7. *Stephanie*

Charlotte couldn't decide if Stephanie's involvement with Cora was another way for her to mess with her and Declan or if she was up to something more sinister. Now that they knew about the bugs in Declan's apartment, it was easy to imagine she'd overheard about the competition between Penny and Tabby, but still, in her heart, she knew Stephanie was more dangerous than anyone suspected.

As she glared at Stephanie's name, she realized visitors to her home who saw Stephanie on that list would think she was out to blame Declan's ex for anything.

But her suspicions had nothing to do with spite or insecurity.

Did they?

She rubbed Stephanie's name away with the side of her hand but left the number seven beside the smear.

I know what it stands for.

As she tossed the chalk back into her drawer, her phone rang, and she answered.

"Charlotte, you have to come. This is *terrible.* Meet me at Juggs right now. I'm already in the car."

It was Penny, and she sounded somewhere between furious and terrified.

"Meet you at...*where*?" Juggs was a restaurant and sports bar known for its top-heavy waitresses. It made similar male-oriented restaurant chains look like five-star dining and was not the sort of place she expected Penny to spend a lot of time.

Penny moaned. "Juggs. Cora's lawyer just called me. She wants Tabby and me to arm wrestle. In public."

"What?"

"She said I had to be at *Juggs* in twenty minutes. Meet me there."

Penny hung up, and Charlotte bolted for the door.

CHAPTER FIFTEEN

Charlotte ran across the street to borrow Mariska's car once again, intending to do so this time with a heartfelt promise to buy her own car as soon as possible. It was finally sinking in that not every case could be solved by golf cart.

She knocked on Mariska's door and explained why she needed the Volkswagen. Mariska's expression registered no surprise as if her friends arm-wrestled at sports bars every day.

"If you think you're going to Juggs to watch Penny arm-wrestle against her sister without me, you're crazy," said Mariska, slipping into her shoes.

"Did you say Juggs?" called her husband Bob from the living room.

"You shush, dirty old man," Mariska called back.

She took a moment to write a text on her ancient phone and then grabbed her keys before leaving.

Charlotte hopped into the car, and Mariska pulled from the driveway and stomped on the gas. A moment later, she slowed down again.

"What are you doing?" asked Charlotte.

"I'm picking up Darla. She'll kill me if I don't."

Ah. That's who she texted. I should have known.

Darla came rolling out of her home. "If you two had gone to this without taking me along, I would have killed you both." She grunted, pretending to try and squeeze into the back seat of the cozy VW Bug.

Charlotte hopped out and motioned to the passenger side. "Darla, sit up front."

"Are you sure?"

She nodded and slipped into the back, which was a little like crawling into a leather coffin. Charlotte was glad she'd picked up on Darla's distress cues. With her bad knees, they would have had to use a crowbar to get Darla back out of the Bug.

Something on the radio caught Charlotte's attention, and she asked Mariska to turn it up.

"...so come out to Juggs today at one, where they'll be holding an old lady arm wrestling competition featuring arm wrestling champion Ricky "The Python" Richards as the referee. Beers will be half price—"

"Stephanie notified the radio stations? How is that possible?" asked Charlotte.

"Oh, Penny is going to *die*," said Darla, barely containing her glee.

Mariska clucked her tongue. "I can't believe Cora is making Penny do all this for that cow-patty-covered patch of grass. I wouldn't pay fifty cents for that land."

"I'm pretty sure arm wrestling wasn't Cora's idea. This has Stephanie written all over it," said Charlotte.

"I used to arm wrestle for drinks. Got pretty good at it, too," said Darla in a dreamy voice.

When they reached Juggs, the small parking lot was overflowing with cars. They spotted Penny pacing at the entrance and pulled into the back to park. They were halfway across the lot when Penny lifted her hands into the air and began jogging towards them.

"What took you so long?" Penny glanced at Mariska and Darla. "And why would you bring *them*?"

"I needed Mariska's car and—"

"You still don't have a car?"

"No, I didn't really need one until—"

"Nevermind. What am I going to do?" Penny grabbed

Charlotte's hand and squeezed it.

Charlotte winced and gently pulled free her hand. "How badly do you want Cow Town?"

"I *have* to get Cow Town."

"Then I guess you're going to arm wrestle your sister."

Penny dropped her head into her hands. "This is so *humiliating*."

Charlotte frowned. "The good news is that I don't think there's any trick to this that we're missing. I can't think of a way that this could be anything but what it seems to be—an opportunity to embarrass you both."

Penny's head popped back up. "Pussy Galore does Pilates. What is that? Does it build muscles?"

Charlotte patted her client on the back and guided her towards Juggs' entrance. "It will all be over in an instant. If you want, let your arm drop and give this one to her. We'll win the next one."

"But she already won the landscaping challenge."

Charlotte grimaced. "That's true. You might want to put a *little* effort into it."

Penny reached toward Mariska and pinched her beefy arm.

"Ow! What is wrong with you?" Mariska pulled away from her.

"Can I use a proxy?" asked Penny.

Charlotte shook her head. "I doubt it."

They slowed as Tabby approached the door from the opposite direction. She wore a blue neoprene brace on her wrist and stretched her shoulders as she walked, dancing like a prize fighter on her way to the ring. A man Charlotte recognized as Edmundo from the landscaping challenge walked beside her.

"That's illegal," said Penny, pointing to her sister's wrist brace.

Tabby jerked her hand behind her back as if to hide it. "It is not."

"We'll see. There are rules. There have to be rules."

"Come, dear, don't waste your energy talking to this riff-raff," said Edmundo, opening the door and ushering Tabby inside. He paused and held out a hand to Charlotte.

"I'm Eddie. You're Charlotte, I presume?"

Charlotte shook his hand and nodded.

"Lovely," said Eddie, winking before he turned and followed his client inside.

"Riff-raff? I'll show you riff-raff," said Darla, holding up a fist as Edmundo retreated.

"He's kind of suave, isn't he?" asked Mariska.

Penny huffed. "I bet Pussy's sleeping with him. She always liked those exotic types."

The four of them entered together, like a gang preparing to take the bar by force. Inside, they worked their way through the crowd, gathering around a tall bar table roped off in the center of the room. Tabby had taken her spot on one of the stools.

Stephanie stood beside her.

The blonde bombshell grinned upon spotting Charlotte and waved toward the empty stool, inviting Penny to take a seat across from her sister. A neoprene mat resembling a giant mouse pad covered the table to provide cushion for the women's bony elbows.

Penny looked at the other three, her eyes wild with fear.

"I can't do this. She'll break my arm, look..."

She pulled up her short sleeve, revealing what looked like a twig wrapped in crepe paper.

Charlotte attempted to console her client. "You're twins, Penny. Look at Tabby. She's built like a bird, too."

"A bird at the end of a hard winter," mumbled Darla.

"You'll be fine," continued Charlotte, gently turning Penny and easing her towards her stool. She sat, and Stephanie elbowed Charlotte back before re-clipping the velvet rope.

"Watch it," said Charlotte.

Stephanie locked eyes with her as the crowd chanted for the competition to begin. "Glad you could make it."

"This is ridiculous, and you know it. You should be ashamed of yourself for creating this spectacle."

Stephanie shrugged. "I'm just carrying out my client's orders."

"Right."

Stephanie offered one last unctuous smile before pointing to the sky with one hand. "Bring out the costumes."

A man burst through the throngs of people with what looked like dresses draped over his outstretched arms. Stephanie spun on her heel and yanked the dresses from him, throwing one to Tabby. The other she held up for the audience to see. The dress unfurled to the ground, and the crowd burst into cheers and a smattering of laughs.

"What is that? Why do they have to wear a dress?" asked Darla.

"It's that book. *The Scarlet Letter,*" said Mariska.

The costumes were black and white puritan-style dresses with a large letter *A* on the chest. Unlike the scarlet letter worn by Hester Prynne in Nathanial Hawthorne's famous novel by that name, this *A* was in the center of the chest and as large as Superman's famous *S*.

Mariska shook her head. "Didn't the *A* in that book stand for—"

"Adulterer," finished Charlotte.

Darla gasped. "Oh. And people would know that?"

"It's one of those books most people have to read in school at some point."

"I must have gone to a terrible school," mumbled Darla.

Mariska placed her hand over her mouth. "This is mortifying. Poor Penny."

Charlotte surveyed the crowd as phone cameras flashed and videos rolled. Cora was nowhere to be seen. As she suspected, Stephanie was running the show.

Charlotte wiggled through the crowd again to get closer to Penny as her client struggled to dress in her costume. As Penny's head popped through the top of the dress, Charlotte placed her hand on her boney arm.

"Don't do this, Penny. Not for a piece of land," she said as quietly as she could and still hope to be heard over the catcalls from the crowd.

Penny looked at her, her eyes rimmed with tears. "You reap

what you sow."

"Penny—"

Penny sniffed and set her jaw, wiping the tears from her eyes with the back of her hand.

"And *I want that land*."

Stephanie moved between Charlotte and Penny. "Return to your seat, please, or you'll be disqualified."

Charlotte glared at her. "You're going to pay for this."

"They actually paid me for bringing in the crowds," said Stephanie before turning to the audience. She thrust her hands over her head, asking for silence.

"Now, I turn you over to your master of ceremonies and referee, two-time Florida state arm wrestling champion, Ricky "The Python" Richards!"

The crowd exploded again, and a short man with biceps as wide as dinner plates stepped forward. "Okay, ladies, take your places."

Stephanie stepped aside to let him into the ring and then melted into the crowd.

Penny and Tabby looked at each other, both seemingly confused as to what their *places* were. Ricky moved in and guided their arms into the right positions, their skeletal fingers wrapped around each other's hands.

"I can't believe Stephanie did all this," said Mariska.

Darla hooted. "I can't believe she hired a real arm wrestler. Look at that man's *arms*. You have to admit that the girl has style."

Charlotte grunted.

Ricky took an extra minute to ensure the sisters were lined up properly and then explained the rules to them and the crowd.

"—touch your opponent's fingers, forearm, or wrist to the table, and you win. You can't use your other hand. All decisions made by me, the referee, are final. Ready?"

The sisters nodded and glowered at each other."

Ricky raised a hand. "Ready...and...*go*!"

For a moment, Charlotte thought that the women had decided against participating. Their entwined hands didn't move one way or the other. It wasn't until she saw the intense grimaces on their faces that she realized they were struggling with all their might but were equally matched.

"Go, Penny!" rooted Mariska.

Momentum swung in Penny's direction before bouncing the other way. Penny's wrist began to bend. After a brief show of force, she appeared helpless to reverse Tabby's attack.

Charlotte knew the end was near.

Apparently, Pilates does make a difference.

Tabby's lips tightened and receded like those of a mummy, her teeth clamped and grinding as she pushed home her win.

Ricky The Python stepped in and lifted Tabby's opposite arm in victory as she bleated at her defeated sister.

"It's mine!" Tabby jumped up and down, clinging to Ricky's arm as if it was her date to the prom. "I won!"

Penny stood and tore her Hester Prynne costume over her head before shoving her way through the crowd and headed for the door.

"I should do this *every* week," yelped a man standing beside Charlotte. He wore a Juggs' staff polo shirt.

"You should be ashamed of yourself," she said.

He laughed. "I am ashamed of myself—for not thinking of this sooner. That blonde is a genius."

Darla and Mariska hustled after Penny, and Charlotte followed. Walking outside, Charlotte squinted beneath the Florida sun as her eyes adjusted from the dark bar.

"Penny," called Mariska, waddling as fast as she could after her neighbor.

"Leave me alone," cried Penny. She tried to open the door of her Cadillac but failed, yelping in pain as she grabbed her shoulder with her opposite hand. Cursing, she opened the door with her good arm.

Mariska, Darla, and Charlotte had to move out of the way as Penny pulled from her parking spot and roared away.

Darla shook her head. "Part of me thought that was hilarious, what with Penny always acting like such a snob, but I do feel bad for her. All those kids in there hollering. It was like a freak show."

"And Penny was the dog-faced boy," said Mariska.

"Tabby didn't seem to mind," said Charlotte.

"Penny's always been the sweet one of those two," said Mariska.

"Penny is the *sweet* one?" echoed Charlotte. She took a moment to wonder what a nightmare Tabby must be. "Were they raised by sharks?"

Speaking of sharks...

She considered storming back inside and giving Stephanie a piece of her mind but knew it would do no good. She silently repeated her mantra.

Sit back and let Stephanie be the crazy one.

The three of them piled back into Mariska's VW and headed for home. Five minutes into the ride, Charlotte's phone chimed.

"Is that a new text noise?" asked Mariska. She was always fascinated by Charlotte's iPhone, though never enough to upgrade from her own clamshell flip phone.

Charlotte shook her head and peered at her screen. "No. It's a motion alert from the video doorbell Declan bought me."

"Oh, what fun. You installed it?"

"No, I didn't. That's what's worrying me." Charlotte pictured the last place she'd seen the doorbell.

Sitting on her kitchen counter.

How is that possible?

She swiped the alert and found the video still rolling. The screen filled with the white of her ceiling and nothing else.

She hit the *talk* button.

"Hey, whoever is in my house, I see you!"

"Who are you talking to?" asked Darla, craning her neck to see.

"I can talk through the doorbell. I'm trying to scare away whoever set it off."

"Someone's in your house?"

"I don't know. I can't see or hear anything."

"Maybe Abby did it somehow?"

"Maybe."

"Do you want me to call Frank?"

"Or I could have Bob cross the street and check on things," suggested Mariska.

"No. We're almost home. I don't want anyone walking in on anything."

Darla jumped in her seat. "Ooh. Maybe it's Declan?"

"Maybe. Good thought." Charlotte called Declan to see if he had stopped by, but he didn't answer. Usually, that meant he was at the shop with a customer.

She spent the remaining ride sitting at the edge of her tiny leather seat, her stomach in knots, concerned she was being robbed but more worried for Abby.

Her connection with the video ended, and she played it from the beginning.

"There," she said.

"What?" chimed the two women in unison.

"There's a flash of something in the video at the beginning, maybe an elbow? It's hard to tell. I can't hear anything."

She replayed it over and over but couldn't even ascertain if it was a male or female elbow—if it was an elbow at all.

Mariska pulled into her driveway, and Charlotte jumped out as fast as she could.

"Don't go running. You don't know who's in there," called Mariska.

Charlotte opened her front door, and Abby ran to her, stubby tail wagging.

"Who was here?" she asked, showering the dog with love.

Abby didn't answer. She didn't seem agitated, either.

Darla and Mariska appeared behind her.

"Is everything okay?"

Charlotte strode through the house, looking for signs of an intruder but found nothing out of place. When she returned from checking the bedroom, she found Darla standing in her kitchen with a knife in her hand.

"Just in case," said Darla.

Charlotte smiled. "If someone was here, it doesn't look like they took anything."

"Was your door still locked?' asked Darla.

"Yes."

"If someone was here, wouldn't Abby have tried to stop them? You would have heard her barking or something."

"I like to think she would have tried. She barks at everyone she doesn't know. I'm thinking it must have been her. She was probably snorfing along the table looking for crumbs—"

Charlotte's gaze settled on her blackboard.

She felt her chest tighten.

"Uh, you guys should go now. I have some work to do. Thank you for the use of your car, as always," she said, carefully sliding the knife from Darla's hand and returning it to her butcher block.

She ushered the women to the door.

"If you see anything amiss, you give me a call, and I'll get Frank over here to check things out," said Darla.

"I will. I promise."

Charlotte waved and closed the door behind them. As soon as they were gone, the smile fell from her lips. She walked to her chalkboard, her gaze dropping to number seven.

In thick red chalk, someone had written a large question mark in the spot next to the digit.

In the *Suspect* slot, she had intentionally left blank.

CHAPTER SIXTEEN

There was only one explanation for the question mark on Charlotte's chalk board.

I'm on to something.

Why else would someone break into her house?

The video doorbell remained on her kitchen counter. She walked by it, hugging tight to the counter edge, and her phone chimed.

If someone had walked by it...

The logical path past the doorbell led directly to her kitchen table, where her computer sat amongst the scattered papers from Bucky's police file. She shifted through them, finding nothing missing.

Her mind wandered to the moment they'd realized Declan's home was bugged. What if *that* was why someone was in her house? To plant bugs?

She made a mental note to keep her mouth shut and straightened the papers, sorting the photos and reports and slipping them back into their package. Popping open the manila envelope, she noticed a small, square object at the bottom of it.

She dumped the envelope upside down and watched a black thumb drive clatter to her table top.

How did I miss this?

She popped the thumb drive into her computer, and a video program auto-loaded. Her screen flickered with what appeared to be security camera footage from Bucky's marina apartment building. The video was a compilation of each person who trigged the camera when entering the building.

Person after person entered. Charlotte groaned and lowered herself into her chair, the burden of proof becoming too heavy to support on two legs. Each unidentified person was a potential lead, but it could take her the rest of her life to divine the identities of *everyone* who entered the marina apartments that day.

She watched as Bucky entered with a dark-haired young woman she recognized as Shawna. That made two people she wouldn't need to identify. She flipped through the rest of the day's footage, but no one else appeared familiar. She dragged a copy of the file to her computer and put the thumb drive back into the folder.

So many leads, and chances were good his death was an accident anyway. All signs pointed to it being an accident.

Except for that chalk question mark.

The question mark on her chalk board gave her both the heebie-jeebies at the idea of someone in her home and hoped that she was on to something.

She rubbed her eyes with the palms of her hands. Becoming obsessed with Bucky's death was distracting her from her real job—winning Cow Town for Penny. She was doing Penny a disservice by not concentrating harder on the individual tests. Was there something she could have done to tip the arm wrestling in Penny's favor? Had she missed a chance?

She couldn't put all her hopes on the big score of unraveling Bucky's possible murder. Penny was down zero to two to her sister.

They needed a win, but only Stephanie knew what was next—

She straightened.

Did it have to be that way?

No.

She needed to get a message to Stephanie, and she knew

just how to do it.

Worried by the possibility of listening devices in her home, Charlotte walked outside and called Seamus.

"Where are you?" she asked when he answered.

"At home."

"You mean Declan's."

"Right. *Home.*"

"Do we still have that roach problem there?"

"Roaches?"

"Bugs."

"Oh, right. Yes."

"I need to give the bugs a message. I'm going to swing by."

"I'll be here. Bring a six-pack."

"What?"

"I'm out."

Charlotte released an exasperated sigh and hung up. She hopped on her bike and pedaled to Declan's house by way of the liquor store.

When she arrived, Seamus answered the door.

"Oh, hello, Charlotte. How are you? What are you doing here?" he said, much too loudly.

She rolled her eyes and covered her ears with her hands to pantomime that he needed a volume adjustment. He nodded, cleared his throat, stretched, and shook his shoulders as if preparing to run a marathon.

"I thought I'd just swing by and talk about the case. Here's your beer." She knew she, too, sounded unnatural, but Seamus had thrown her out of her rhythm.

He took the six-pack. "Oh good, thanks, come on in. Want one?"

"No, thank you."

"It's Saturday."

"I know. But no, thank you."

He shrugged and pulled a can from its plastic harness. "Fine then. More for me."

She took a moment to collect herself. Seamus' awkwardness was making her performance for the bugs much more difficult than she'd anticipated. "So, *anyway*, I just got back from an arm-wrestling match."

"With who?"

"Not me. Stephanie called Penny and Tabby and demanded they meet at Juggs, where she'd arranged for a huge arm-wrestling match. She made them compete in front of the whole bar while wearing a scarlet *A* costume."

"A what?"

She pointed to her chest. "Like *The Scarlet Letter*—that novel where a puritan woman is forced to wear a bright red letter *A* on her dress, so the whole town knows she was an adulterer."

"Jaysis."

"Yeah. Pretty harsh. But you know, it's just like Stephanie to pick on Penny."

Seamus stared at her, and she waved her hand around like a motor gear, encouraging him to play along.

"Oh yeah?" he asked.

"Absolutely. Stephanie doesn't have the *guts* to pick on you or me. She has to pick on old women."

Seamus grinned, and Charlotte could see he was catching on. "You're right. It's sad, really, that she never gives us the chance to beat her. Such a frightened little girl she is."

"It is sad. That's the perfect word for it. Almost as sad as her thinking she's going to get Declan back."

Seamus laughed and then slapped his hand over his mouth as he tried to rein in his unbridled mirth.

"And how about how she came crawling back here to Charity? How sad is *that*? Who knows what embarrassments she suffered out in the big wide world that she had to come home and lick her wounds?"

"Good point," Seamus peeped before again covering his mouth. His body shook with silent laughter.

"Don't even get me started on her mother—"

Seamus's eyes grew wide. "I have to get the paper. I'll be right back." He bolted out the front door.

"That's okay. I should probably be going anyway," she said

to no one but the bugs.

She went outside to find Seamus staring at her with his jaw hanging as low as it could fall.

"Are you crazy?"

"Why?"

Seamus scratched his head and began to pace. "I mean, I understand you're trying to get her to punt us one of the challenges, but there's stirring up the hornet's nest, and then there's slipping it over your head."

"Is that a saying in Ireland?"

He paused and cocked his head. "What? *No.* I don't think so—you know what I mean."

"You think I should be scared of her."

"Yes. It's like she has more hours in a day than the rest of us and she spends them all planning terrible things. And for you to bring up her mother. That woman is a killer. Literally."

Charlotte rolled her eyes. "They didn't seem that close the last time we saw them together."

"They're *mother and daughter*. You can't break that bond. Maybe Mommy wishes they were closer. Ever think of that? Maybe she thinks Stephanie would love her more if she gift-wrapped us and chopped up into little pieces."

Charlotte laughed. "I wanted her to focus on us. I figured the easiest way to do it would be to dent that enormous ego of hers and get her angry at you and me."

"Yeah, thanks for the warning on that one. Now I'm in the line of fire."

"We can handle her."

Seamus shook his head and sighed. "I hope you're right. I don't think that apple fell far from the nutter tree in that family."

Charlotte smiled. "I think we'll find out very soon."

CHAPTER SEVENTEEN

Charlotte had barely returned home from her meeting with Seamus before her text alert bleeped.

She looked at her phone and smiled.

Stephanie.

It hadn't taken long to get that psycho's attention. The prompt response to Charlotte's taunting confirmed that she was responsible for the bugs in Declan's house.

She read the text message.

Meet me at Cow Town. Just you.

The location was convenient. Cow Town sat directly behind Pineapple Port, separated by little more than a swampy ditch of trees and brush.

It had already been a long day. Charlotte gave Abby a treat to apologize for being away so much, pulled her hair back into a ponytail, and headed for Cow Town.

She picked her way through the sticker bush-laden, shallow ravine and emerged on the other side next to a fence that encircled an open field. Across from where she stood, she could see Stephanie's red Viper parked against the opposite fence, waiting like a vibrant but deadly dart frog.

Cows lifted their heads from their grazing and watched her as she crossed the field, picking her way around droppings both new and old. She regretted not changing from flip-flops to sneakers almost immediately but didn't feel like going all the way back to the house.

Halfway through the field, she spotted a second car pulling next to the first. This one was an old yellow Mustang. The field was starting to resemble a classic car show.

A man emerged from the Mustang, and she recognized him as Edmundo, still wearing the same clothes he'd worn at the arm wrestling event.

Stephanie got out of her car and walked over to shake hands with Edmundo.

Charlotte felt an uneasy feeling creeping up her neck. She was here. Edmundo was here…

She couldn't have planned another test already.

She slipped through the fence and approached the other two.

"Charlotte, I believe you've met Edmundo? He's working for Tabby."

Eddie thrust out his hand and smiled. "It's nice to meet you again. You can call me Eddie. And let me lend you my deepest condolences that you find yourself working with Seamus."

Charlotte chuckled and shook his hand. "Nice to meet you."

Stephanie crossed her arms over her chest and cocked her hip. "Now that we've gotten the niceties out of the way, I have a challenge for you. A chance to win one for your side."

Stephanie locked her gaze on Charlotte. "After all, we can't let the old ladies have all the fun."

Charlotte did her best to show no reaction, but one thing was clear.

Stephanie knew her bugs were blown.

A huge horse trailer turned off the road and backed into the part of the lot that stood outside the fenced area. It stopped ten feet from where they were standing, and another trailer followed, parking in front of the first.

Stephanie smiled. "You know, the man who uses this land for grazing was *so* pleased when I told him I'd pack up his cows for him."

Charlotte looked out into the field and then down at her flip-flops. "You want us to put those cows into those trailers?"

Stephanie nodded. “Whoever puts more cows in the trailers wins.”

Eddie shook his head and motioned to his suit. “I cannot do this. At the very least, I need to change first.”

Stephanie shrugged. “You can change—if you want Charlotte to get an impossible lead on you.”

“No, no. You’ve made a mistake. I am here to investigate Bucky’s murder for Tabby. Not to play farmer.”

Stephanie shrugged. “Then you can tell Tabby she lost this one.”

Eddie rubbed his tongue against his cheek for several moments and then shook his head.

“No. I will not do this. I am an investigator. Not a farmer.” He nodded to each of them and returned to his car to leave.

Stephanie lolled her head in Charlotte’s direction. “He’s not a farmer, in case you didn’t catch that.”

“I guess I win by default?”

Stephanie laughed. “After you remove the cows from the pasture, yes.”

Charlotte put her hand on her chest. “By myself? But I only need *one* to officially beat Eddie.”

“They all have to go in, or the contest is null and void.”

“You’re making up these rules as you go along.”

Stephanie nodded. “Yep.”

Charlotte turned and stared at the cows. It would be nice to walk away and leave Stephanie with the cows to move. But she’d already lost the first competition. She needed a win.

She closed her eyes and hung her head. “Fine. Do you have a lead or something I can use?”

Stephanie squinted at her. “A what?” A large, black pickup truck with *Swick Excavation* on the door pulled up at the opposite end of the field. “I have to go. Have at it.”

She waved at the field and walked off, hardly wobbling in her heels, even on the rough path that ran along the fence line.

I can’t stand her.

The man who had driven the first trailer opened the back gate, and Charlotte asked for a spare lead she could borrow. He had one, so she took it and headed out to the field to find her first cow.

Clipping the lead onto the halter of the first cow, she pulled the animal toward the gate. The cow's neck stretched forward, but her cloven hooves didn't move.

"Oh, please don't do this to me," begged Charlotte. She reached for the cow's rump to slap some encouragement into it but found she couldn't pull it forward and urge it on from behind at the same time.

She heard the sound of an engine and turned to see Eddie's yellow Mustang pulling up beside the trailers.

He's back.

He hopped out of the car and strode to the gate.

"I am not a quitter," he announced, pointing his finger to the sky.

Charlotte's shoulders slumped. She hadn't moved one cow a single foot forward before the competition returned. She grabbed the cow's halter and tugged, clucking her tongue and making every noise she could imagine might encourage a cow.

"I'll give you a big stick of butter if you come with me," she cooed before realizing cows make butter. They don't eat it. "What am I saying? Hey, how about a hamburger?"

The cow stepped forward, and she whooped with joy.

"You're a cannibal. Who knew?"

Once she'd made the cow move, momentum commenced, and the beast continued walking toward the gate. She found it helped to stay beside its head, holding the lead short rather than pulling it like a tug-of-war rope.

She passed Eddie as he stormed toward the next-closest cow.

"Couldn't just give up, huh?" she asked.

"Not after Tabby offered me another thousand to stay. I can buy two suits for that money."

Charlotte grimaced and walked faster. She was going to have to talk to Penny about a bonus for this one.

The trailer driver stationed himself on the wheel well with a clipboard and a pen. As she walked her cow toward the ramp and into the trailer, he slashed a mark on what she assumed was her side of the paper.

One down. One million to go.

She clipped Bessie to the wall of the trailer and jogged out to find a second.

Stephanie had been standing at the fence watching and talking to the man who'd arrived in the black pickup. Charlotte was staring at her when she waved and got into the truck. The two of them drove away.

"Where is she going?" she asked, trotting past Eddie, who was walking in the opposite direction, dragging a slow cow.

"Far away, I hope," said Eddie. His gaze lingering on the retreating pickup, he stepped into a soft patch of ground. The pasture was largely dry but had low pockets of moisture from the previous night's rain. Charlotte heard a sucking sound as Eddie lost one of his loafers in the mud. He cursed.

She giggled all the way to the next cow.

Bessie Two followed without struggle, and Charlotte reached the trailer seconds behind Eddie as he clipped in his latest.

"Did you know Stephanie before?" asked Charlotte, snapping in her own beast. She and Eddie fell into pace together as they returned to the field.

"I met her one month ago. She was down in Miami asking questions about Seamus. Her path led her to me since I have known that man a very long time."

"She was asking questions about Seamus?" Charlotte scowled. She couldn't think of any reason for Stephanie to be investigating Seamus' past other than an attempt to find dirt on him; that she could later use against him. Seamus had admitted to her and Declan that he'd worked undercover for the Miami police, providing them with information and materials they couldn't retrieve legally. That occupation sounded ripe with gray areas.

She made a mental note to warn Seamus.

The two of them split to retrieve separate cows, and Charlotte began to run in an attempt to secure her lead. She heard Eddie muttering.

"Don't do that. I'm too old to keep up with you."

Charlotte laughed. "That's what I'm hoping."

CHAPTER EIGHTEEN

As the sun began to dip, Charlotte resented the cow-shuffling chore even more. Eddie removed his shirt and tied it around his head to keep the sweat from his eyes, treading back and forth in his soaking wet, white tank undershirt.

"It's starting to feel like we'll never finish," said Charlotte as she clipped in a cow, and the driver marked his tally.

"She just called, so you'll be done soon," said the driver.

Charlotte paused, leaned her hands on her knees, and attempted to catch her breath.

"She just called?"

"Yeah. This is the craziest thing I've ever seen."

"Making a guy in a suit and a girl in flip flops load cows?"

"No, circulating cows."

Charlotte scowled. "Is that what you call taking them away to another pasture?"

The man laughed. "No, that's what I call driving them around the dogleg and sending them back *into* the pasture."

Charlotte straightened. "What did you say?"

"See the dog leg up there?" The man pointed to where the pasture took a right turn around another neighborhood and disappeared.

Charlotte knew the turn well—she'd been dreading it. They hadn't even started to work their way around the corner, and she feared how many cows might be lurking there. "Yes?"

"You've been bringing the cows from this end of the field into the truck, and then we drive them around the block and send them back in the other end. Once they're back in, she had us scoot them down this way so you wouldn't notice.

Charlotte's jaw fell. "You're saying we've been packing up the same cows over and over?"

"Yep. Did you think a forty acre pasture could hold a hundred cows?"

"I don't know how many cows an acre can hold."

The man spat. "'bout two dozen."

Eddie arrived with a cow and stopped.

"What's wrong with you?" he asked.

"They're not taking the cows away. They're driving them around the corner and re-releasing them into the pasture."

"What?" Eddie looked at the cow lead in his hand. "I thought this one looked familiar."

The driver spat again. "Yeah, well, it's over now. Boss-lady called and said to start taking them to the new pasture."

Furious, Charlotte pounded past Eddie and back into the pasture. Feeling as though her gait was off, she lifted her foot and found a build-up of cow dung had attached itself to her flip-flop. She pulled it off, her lip curled with disgust.

Standing straight, she was about to toss the dried clump back into the field when she noticed Stephanie's car parked next to the fence. The windows were down to keep it ventilated.

A smile oozed across her face.

Hauling back, Charlotte threw the dried dung in the direction of the open window. It arced neatly and disappeared within the vehicle.

"I saw that," said Eddie, approaching.

Charlotte felt her face flush with embarrassment, but Eddie grinned. He dipped down and retrieved his own dry chunk of cow dung.

"One for each cow, eh?" He lobbed a piece, and it flew through the center of the Viper's open widow, a perfect shot.

Charlotte held out her hand. "Deal."

They shook.

The two trailers had circulated many times, each holding a dozen cows before driving away to return in time to be loaded again. Charlotte had lost count of how many cows she'd taken into the trailer, and she hoped Eddie had as well. He didn't seem to be moving as fast as he had been. Either he knew he had lost, or he was confident of his lead.

For the remaining twenty cows, they each tossed a piece of dung into the open window of the Viper.

Suddenly, the job didn't seem so bad.

The pickup truck that had taken Stephanie away reappeared. The driver handed her his clipboard tally and then drove off with the last of the bovines.

"You two look a little sweaty. Eddie, I don't think that suit will ever be the same."

"Just tell us who won," said Eddie, wiping his brow."

Stephanie looked over the tally, pulled her phone from her purse, and dialed.

"Hi, Cora? I thought you'd like to know who won the cow challenge."

Charlotte swallowed with difficulty. Her throat was dry, and she was exhausted. Foreboding washed over her.

Regardless of the tally, she found it hard to believe that Stephanie would allow her to win.

"The winner is..." Stephanie looked at them and paused for dramatic effect.

"Charlotte. She won by two cows."

Charlotte yelped with joy. Eddie hung his head for a second and then headed for his car.

"Sorry, Eddie. It's been nice working with you," Charlotte called after him without a hint of sarcasm.

Eddie winked and slipped into his Mustang before roaring off.

Stephanie dropped her phone back into her purse and, without another word, sauntered towards her car.

Uh oh. Time to go.

Charlotte slipped through the fence and started across the field at a good clip. She made it all the way to the scrub brush separating the field from Pineapple Port when she heard Stephanie scream.

She grinned.

The victory had been sweet, but the dung had been sweeter.

Walking to her house with a new spring in her step, she noticed a white cat sitting on the window sill of her neighbor's house. Her thoughts ran back to Johnnie Walker Cat.

Poor thing.

Frank wouldn't have his warrant until Monday if he was even able to get it then. In the meantime, that miserable store owner could ditch evidence, cover his tracks...

She sighed. She was so tired, but—

She hopped in the shower at home and, toweling off, checked the clock to find it was nearly seven.

Declan had finished work and was probably at home.

She grabbed her phone and called him. Seamus answered.

"Why are you answering Declan's cell phone?" she asked.

"Hello to you, too," said Seamus.

"Sorry, hello."

"He's in the shower."

"Ah. That's okay. I needed to talk to you too."

"Really? How exciting."

"Do you still have that bug sweeper?"

"Yes."

"Good. I need you to check my house. Someone was in here, and it could have been Stephanie pulling the same trick she did on Declan."

"How do you know someone was in there?"

"My video doorbell captured movement in the house. I set it up but hadn't hung it outside yet."

"Really? But you can't tell who it was?"

"No. It caught the flash of an elbow, maybe. Can you do it tonight?"

"Sure. I'll swing over in a little bit."

"Great. I'll leave the door open for you. Abby knows you. Ignore her if she barks."

"I'm not afraid of that fluff muffin."

"Oh, and you can remove the bugs you found at Declan's."

"Why's that?"

"I just saw Stephanie. She knows we know."

"Where? How?"

"I was barely back from seeing you when she called and put Eddie and me head-to-head in a cow-clearing challenge. We emptied Cow Town, like, twenty times over."

"Oh yeah? You beat the schmuck?"

"I did. Barely. I have to say, he seemed really nice."

"Och. Don't let him fool you."

Charlotte chuckled. "We threw cow dung in Stephanie's car. One piece for each cow."

"How cute. Invite me to the wedding."

"Ha. Oh, and I found out why he's here. Stephanie went to Miami to ask around about *you* and met him there."

"Ask about me? That doesn't sound good. I'll have to ask around and find out more. Oh, wait, here's your boyo. Hold on."

A moment later, Declan's voice came on the line. "Hello?"

Charlotte braced herself to do some heavy-duty convincing. "I need you for a very important mission."

Declan sighed. "I hate it when you say that."

CHAPTER NINETEEN

Charlotte crouched in the dirt and found a direct line of sight to the Quickie Stop convenience store's back door. The view was clear, but for a few sticks and leaves. She'd stationed Declan around the corner to keep an eye on the front of the store. Given a choice between hiding in the bushes in the dirt or sitting in his car, he'd chosen his car.

Shocker.

Though, that was how she'd planned it all along. Declan needed to be in the more visible spot since Cody, the Quickie Stop owner, had seen her with Frank that morning.

Her phone buzzed, and she glanced at it.

We're totally sure this is necessary? asked Declan via text.

She hit the text message microphone and murmured an answer into the phone. *Yes. Frank can't get a search warrant until Monday. Is Cody still in there?*

Yes. But he looks like he's closing up.

Good.

Her phone went silent for several minutes and then buzzed again.

He turned off all the lights, wrote Declan.

Has he come out the front?

No. Remember when we would have had to do this with walkie-talkies?

Not really.

Me neither. But if Frank was here, you can bet he'd be telling us all about it.

She laughed out loud and then covered her mouth to squelch the noise. No wonder detectives were always so hard-boiled. Laughing could get you caught.

Another ten minutes went by, and Charlotte began to worry that Cody lived above his store like Mr. French. They could stake the place all evening, only to watch him jog downstairs and start all over again in the morning.

A clatter made her jump. Crouching lower, she watched as Cody rolled open the garage door at the back of the store. She wanted to text Declan an update but feared she'd miss something.

Cody disappeared into the dark depths of what appeared to be a storage room, and she tapped out a message.

He opened the back garage door.

He's leaving?

IDK. He went back in. I'll let you know.

She spotted movement and turned her phone to airplane mode. She couldn't risk a buzzing phone alerting her suspect.

A large white box was wheeled from the garage bay. Once it cleared the door, she could see Cody had what appeared to be a large freezer on a dolly. He rolled it to the parking area behind the store, opened the back of a black Ford pickup truck, and, with great effort and grunting, slid the appliance into the bed.

She noted the freezer had a cloth strap around it to keep the lid from falling open.

Or to keep a body from knocking it open.

It couldn't be a coincidence that the day Frank threatened him with a search warrant, Cody decided to move a freezer under the cover of darkness. Johnnie Walker Cat couldn't be wrong.

Poor Mr. French *had* to be in that freezer.

She had a decision to make. Proving Cody had killed Mr. French would be a lot harder without a body.

I can't let him get away.

Charlotte crept to the thickest bush closest to the truck.

Cody turned to pull down the garage door, and she leaned from the bushes, intending to hop into the truck or tap the freezer for signs of life.

With an eloquent economy of movement, Cody flung closed the door and whirled back toward the truck. Charlotte retracted into the bushes and stopped breathing until she heard him enter the Ford.

The truck roared to life, and on impulse, she sprinted from her hiding place to grab the back of the vehicle, her feet on the bumper. Staying low and clinging like a refrigerator magnet, she waited until he shifted into drive. Hoping his eyes would be trained on the road like a conscientious driver, she spilled over the hatch and into the bed of the truck. The freezer slid toward her, pinning her to the hatch as if it had been desperately searching for a cuddle partner for some time.

Charlotte took short, choppy breaths until Cody made a left turn and the freezer slid away, releasing her.

Wedging her leg against the appliance to keep it from sliding, she tapped against the side of it.

"Mr. French? Are you in there?" she called as loud as she dared.

The truck's engine roared, and she realized she couldn't be sure if Mr. French was calling to her or not.

She knew the rules. If a television mystery show lasted more than a season or two, someone eventually suffocated in a freezer. Just like every long-standing sitcom featured someone giving birth in an elevator.

Television tropes were tropes for a reason.

I have to break the seal.

The truck pulled off the paved road and onto a dirt path. Jostling from the wheel well to hatch and back, she opened her lock pick case and retrieved a small knife for sawing at the strap securing the lid.

"I'm coming, Mr. French."

After sawing for what felt like an eternity and after vowing to buy sharper knives over a dozen times, the strap gave way. Positioning her foot against the lower lip of the seal, she jerked on the lid.

She smelled it before she felt it.

A wave of liquid burst from the freezer like the faltering of a dam, soaking her to the bone with viscous gunk.

Though she couldn't see well enough to tell the color, she knew the liquid could only be one thing.

Blood.

The truck slowed to a halt.

CHAPTER TWENTY

Declan abandoned texting and pressed Charlotte's saved number on his phone. He didn't want to compromise her with phone noise, but it had been nearly twenty minutes. The last thing she'd said was that Cody was on the move, and now she wouldn't answer. He knew she wasn't one to back down.

What had she gotten herself into?

Her voicemail message played.

That's it.

He didn't care if he blew the whole operation. He had to check on her.

Declan stepped out of his car and slipped into the alley between the convenience store and the apartment next door. He jogged the length of it and peered around the corner.

Nothing.

He crept a little farther and saw that the store's garage door was closed.

"Charlotte?" he whispered into the night.

No response.

He moved closer to the bushes where she'd planned to lay in wait.

"Charlotte?"

Silence.

Declan stared at the rolling door at the back of the store. The last thing she'd said was that the door was *opening*.

What if she'd confronted him, and he'd pulled her inside?

He moved to the door and rapped on it with his knuckles. "Charlotte?"

He thought he heard something and knocked again, louder.

There. A grunting noise echoed from behind the door.

Banging more authoritatively, he heard the moaning grow louder and more consistent.

"Charlotte?"

Another sound. It wasn't *unlike* a muffled scream.

She's definitely trying to respond. He jerked on the door but found it locked. Beside the rolling door was a rickety, standard-issue wooden door. Declan rammed his shoulder into it and felt the frame shudder. He kicked to the right of the knob several times, but the lock held.

It would help to not be wearing flip-flops.

Stupid Florida.

Gritting his teeth, he ran at the door, and it cracked. Pounding at the weakened center, he pulled enough splinters away to reach in and unlock the door from the inside.

"Charlotte!"

A moan echoed from the opposite side of the cavernous room behind the rolling door. Declan found and flipped a light switch, but it illuminated outside instead of inside.

"I'm coming!" he plunged toward the moans, tripping against piles of soft drink flats and boxes of snack chips in the dim illumination provided by the outside lamp. The windows of the rolling door had been largely painted black, with only dots of light shining through.

The pleas emanating from the darkest corner of the room grew more frenzied the closer he drew. As it became harder to see, he reached out until his groping hand dropped into the lap of the frantic hostage.

Reaching upward, he found a face and peeled what felt like duct tape from the mouth.

"*Ow*! My mustache!"

Though the voice was high with panic, Declan knew he'd stumbled upon a *man*, not his damsel in distress. Charlotte sometimes let her legs go for a few days, but she'd never had a mustache.

"Who are you?" asked Declan.

"I'm Robert French. Get me out of here—he's going to kill me! He'll kill us both!"

"Who?"

"Cody. The idiot who owns this dirty little hole-in-the-wall."

"Did you see a girl?"

"What?"

Declan leaned forward and grabbed the hysterical man by his shirt. *"Did you see a girl?"*

"No. Why? Did he kidnap a girl, too?"

Declan released a sharp, frustrated sigh. "Hold on."

Eyes adjusting to the dim illumination, Declan located another light switch and flicked it on.

Mr. French sat squiggling in the corner, tied to a chair. His clothing was torn and dirty, and he had small round wounds on his arms.

Charlotte was nowhere to be seen.

Declan retrieved his phone and called Frank as he headed to search the front of the store. He could barely hear with Mr. French demanding his return to the warehouse.

"It's midnight. This better be good," answered Frank.

"It's Declan. He's got Charlotte."

"What? *Who*?"

Declan paced as he spoke. "We were staking out the convenience store, and Cody came out the back, and now she's gone, and Mr. French is tied to a chair in the back of the store."

Frank started a sentence several times without getting past the first consonant. Finally, Declan heard him sputter a curse beneath his breath. "Stay there. I'm on my way. *Don't move*."

CHAPTER TWENTY-ONE

Charlotte tried to think about anything other than the stench that clung to every inch of her. Lying in the bed of the truck, the trapped pool of blood sloshed back and forth over her like a putrid tide.

She heard Cody put his truck into park.

There was no time to escape.

Cody exited the cab.

I'm going to barf. I'm definitely going to barf.

Cody's upper body bobbed along the side of the truck bed, and he hooted as the smell within reached his nostrils. He opened the back gate as gallons of liquid escaped out onto his shoes.

"Son of a—" He raised his chin, and his gaze met Charlotte's. "Who are *you*?"

Charlotte's fingers fell upon something wet and meaty. Her struggle to *not* barf ceased to be a winnable game.

She retched, and Cody leapt back with a yelp of disgust.

Taking the opportunity to escape, she crawled as fast as she could from the back of the truck, dry heaving as she went. Stumbling, she started down the dirt road away from Cody and his Truck of Horrors.

"Hey! Hey!" she heard Cody calling behind her.

She tried to move faster but had to drop to her knees as nausea again overtook her. The stench of the blood had robbed her of any ability to control her gag reflex.

"Who are you? What were you doing in the back of my truck?" Cody demanded.

Hunched on the ground, Charlotte turned her head to look back at him, her blood-soaked hair flopping across her face. She tried to speak but found she couldn't.

Cody stomped his foot. "Were you there when I slid the freezer in? Are you drunk? High?" He took a step towards her and then jerked back. "Oh—" He gagged and stepped backward and away from her.

Charlotte realized that covered in blood like a wet rat and lying in the dark, Cody couldn't recognize her. She curled into a fetal position and nodded.

"Tequila," she croaked, sliding her knife from her pocket. Pretending to heave, which wasn't hard, she opened the blade and held it hidden, ready to defend herself. Even *not* covered in blood and sick to her core, the odds weren't good that she'd be able to outrun Cody. He didn't look a day over thirty and was built like a whippet.

"The booze isn't the worst of your problems now, you stupid bitch," he said, laughing. He found a spot to stand equally far from her and the blood-covered truck.

Charlotte glared at him through her straggly hair, wondering how she could have missed such a prince among men when she was single.

Ah, what could have been.

He put his hands on his hips. "I gotta dump this spoiled meat, go spray out the freezer—and now spray out the damn truck, too, thanks to you. You thank your lucky stars for that stink, or I'd teach you a lesson you'd never forget."

Charlotte nodded.

Charming. Wait—Did he say spoiled meat?

Charlotte's gaze drifted back to the truck. *Was he lying? Or was it really beef and not Mr. French?*

"It's meat?" she echoed.

"Yeah, it's *meat*. What the hell else would it be? Damn thing broke with nearly a whole deer my buddy'd given me inside."

She heaved again.

Cody removed his flannel shirt and tied it over his mouth and nose. By the glow of the truck's parking lights, she could see his right arm was covered with what looked like thin scratches.

Cat scratches. No wonder the cat hated him and his bell—Johnnie Walker Cat had been there when Cody presumably attacked his owner and tried to stop him with his two remaining feet.

Jerking the freezer from the truck bed, Cody dumped it into the grass before sliding it back into place.

He pulled the shirt from his face and pointed at her as he headed for the driver's side.

"You stay away from my truck from now on, y'hear? Or that won't be *deer* blood on you next time—it'll be yours."

A moment later, he was gone.

Charlotte pulled her phone from her pocket and called Declan.

He groaned with relief. "Charlotte, where are you?"

"I have no idea, but I'm covered in deer blood. At least, I hope I am, and he wasn't lying."

"What? You had us worried sick."

"Us?"

"Frank is here. I went looking for you and found Mr. French tied up in the back of the store."

"He's alive? Ooh—I can't *tell* you how happy I am to hear that. I thought I was covered in French dip."

"What?"

"Bad joke. Nevermind."

"Charlotte, where *are* you?"

"I really don't know. Some dirt road."

"How is that possible? Did he grab you? Are you okay?"

"I'm fine. I hid in the back of his truck, and he drove to the middle of nowhere to dump a freezer full of spoiled meat. I thought he had Mr. French in the freezer."

"Are you safe now?"

"Yes. He left. Found me covered in spilled freezer blood and ran away as fast as possible."

"He left you—" Declan paused. "Ah. *French dip.* I get it now. That's disgusting."

"The deer dip isn't exactly Chanel Number Five either. Is Frank still there?"

"Yes, he's standing right here. They took Mr. French away. He was covered in cigarette burns. Cody tortured him until he agreed to sell him his store. Made him sign papers and said he was going to kill him."

"Yikes. I guess that makes sense. Cody's angling for a Seven-Eleven franchise, and he needs a better location. French's store would be perfect.

"Heck of a way to get a space."

As they spoke, Charlotte crawled to her feet and made her way down the dirt road. She noticed a small pond and found herself transfixed by it.

"Charlotte? Are you still there?" asked Declan.

"Oh. Sorry. Yes. I'm trying to decide whether I'd rather continue to smell like death or be eaten by an alligator."

"Don't do anything stupid. I'm on my way to my car."

"Wait—give your phone to Frank. I have to tell him something."

She heard Declan sharing a synopsis of her situation before Frank's gruff baritone drowned all else. "Frank here. Little lady, you and I are going to have to have a serious talk about making smart decisions."

Charlotte chuckled. "I'm not in a position to disagree. But Frank, listen, I keep wondering why Cody would decide to house clean in the middle of the night. I think he's headed back to put Mr. French, dead or alive, in the freezer and get him out of there before you show up with a warrant. You can grab him if you don't spook him."

It was silent while Frank processed the information. A moment later, he began barking orders at the other policemen to clear the area. Declan's voice returned.

"What did you tell him?" he asked.

"I think Cody's on his way back to put Mr. French in his empty freezer."

Declan sighed, and she heard his car door close.

"I'm tracking your phone. Hang up before it dies. I'll be there as soon as I can. Then you and I are going to have a talk, too."

She smiled, happy that he cared. "Have I been bad? Are you going to spank me?" She'd barely spoken the words before she felt her face grow warm with a flush of embarrassment.

His voice fell soft. "It's not funny, Char. I was really scared."

"I'm sorry. I really am." She paused and then couldn't help herself. "I know that was *cheeky* of me to say."

He snorted a laugh. "You're hopeless. Hang up. I love you."

"Fine. I love you, too."

She disconnected and continued down the road. After four steps, she stopped.

Wait. Did he just say I love you?

Did I?

She grinned until she tasted blood and then spat and heaved. She gave up trying to make progress towards nowhere and sat in the dirt.

Declan found Mr. French, Frank will catch Cody, Johnnie Walker Cat solved the case—and I'll never be able to eat venison again.

Her phone dinged, and she looked at it to find a text from Seamus. He'd completed his sweep of her house and found no bugs. That was something, at least.

Though if he had found listening devices, she would have known who was in her house and why. As it was, the flashing elbow remained a mystery.

CHAPTER TWENTY-TWO

Abby bounded down the hallway to greet Charlotte and Declan as they entered her house. Rounding the corner, the dog screeched to a halt as the aroma of Charlotte's blood bath filled her flaring nostrils.

She'd done her best to towel off the worst of the mess before getting into Declan's car, but trying to sneak deer blood past a dog's nose was like trying to tiptoe on creaky floors past a bat.

Abby ignored Declan and slammed her nose into Mommy, sniffing with the intensity of a car vacuum. She found the mother lode of yumminess on Charlotte's shorts and began trying to eat them.

"Oh, Abby. Get away. That's disgusting." She looked at Declan. "I need to—"

"Get a shower. Yes. This I know. I'll be outside burning my passenger seat."

Charlotte scooted to her room, Abby scrabbling tight on her heels.

She couldn't remember a time a shower felt so good, and as a bonus, it gave her an excuse to use her unwanted collection of fragrant soaps. Retirement community people were always pushing perfumy toiletries on each other, no matter what the occasion. Birthday? Lily-of-the-valley soap. Christmas? Pine-scented bath gel. President's Day? Enjoy a lavender loofa.

She never could figure out why anyone would want to smell like a Christmas tree, but she was thrilled to obliterate the smell of rotting deer blood with *Rose Petal Riot*.

Slipping into some comfortable clothes, she tossed her clothes into a plastic bag and ran them out to the trash. There would be no saving them.

When she returned, Abby sniffed her over and then parked herself in front of the door, just in case something delicious crawled back inside.

Charlotte found Declan at her kitchen table, picking through Bucky's case file.

"This stuff is pretty gruesome," he said, flipping over the photos of Bucky's autopsy.

"I know. They had Frank swearing to be cremated. Do you want some wine?"

"Sure. Maybe one to get my shoulders to un-bunch before I head back. Hey, I never did ask how things went with your Bucky investigation today."

She sighed as she poured two glasses of merlot. "Terrible. I didn't find anything, oh, except this."

She slipped a Tupperware container from the top of the refrigerator as Declan retrieved his glass. Unsealing the plastic box, she held it out so he could inspect the stinky substance she'd found on the roof deck.

Declan jerked away. "Ugh. That smells almost as bad as you."

"I took a shower."

"I mean before."

"Mm." Charlotte caught a whiff of the putrid mass, and the little spark that had first flared to life upon finding it, this time fanned into a flame.

"*Potato*!" she barked as if it were a profanity.

Declan chuckled. "*Potato*? Is that what the retirees say instead of cursing now?"

"No, it's *potato*. I thought there was something familiar about this stink. It's rotten, raw *potato*."

"How'd you come up with that?"

"I keep my potatoes up here on the fridge in this basket, and every once in a while, I lose track of one, and *whew!* They do *not* go gently into that dark night. I can tell you that."

"Huh. How weird."

She resealed the Tupperware. "You're Irish. Isn't knowing potatoes in every state of being bred into your blood from birth?"

"Very funny. Actually, I *am* a potato freak, you have me there, but I've never tried fermenting them on my fridge before."

"All the kids are doing it."

"I bet."

Charlotte slid the container back on top of her refrigerator.

"So what does that mean?" asked Declan, handing her the other glass of wine.

"What? The fact that there was potato at the crime scene?"

He nodded.

She shrugged. "I don't know. Nothing, I'm sure. Probably, some bird dropped it. Stole it from some restaurant's trash or something."

"Are you going to take it to the police for testing?"

"A pile of stinky goo? They'd laugh me out of the precinct. I think I only kept it so I could feel like I'd done something useful."

Charlotte grimaced. Something Declan had said a moment before struck her as odd.

"Hey…when I realized that gunk was potato, you said *How weird* in an odd, sort of wry, way. Almost like it was ironically *not* weird. Why did you say that?"

"Did I? You read that much into the phrase *how weird*?"

She nodded.

He wandered back to the kitchen table. "Well, for one, it's weird finding potato at a crime scene, but you're right, there was more to it. When you went to get a shower, I hopped on your computer to check my email and saw these pictures. Does this girl have something to do with the case?"

He woke the laptop and pointed to the screen as he slid into a chair. Charlotte peered over his shoulder.

"That's Shawna's Instagram page—the girl Bucky was with when he died."

"*That's* the girl Bucky was with? Oh my."

"I know. She's a tad young for him. Anyway, she was the only one with him when it happened, but she didn't *see* it happen. She was down in his apartment, according to her."

"But you think she had something to do with it?"

"Possibly, but I don't get a bad vibe from her. I keep thinking she might know more than she *knows* she knows, though, you know?"

"I *know*." He chuckled as he rolled through the feed and then gestured to the screen. "Here. It was this."

Declan pointed to the photo she'd seen earlier of Shawna and her brother Dallas. He tapped on the image of a long black tube leaning against Dallas' pile of junk from college.

"What? Is that something special? I figured it was some kind of sports equipment."

"You really don't know what it is?"

"No. Should I?"

He thought for a moment. "I guess not."

She shook his shoulder in frustration. "Well, what *is* it?"

He leaned back in his chair, crossed his arms over his chest, and cocked an eyebrow. "What's my cut if I tell you?"

"One kiss."

"Two and we have a deal."

She pecked him twice on the lips.

He smiled. "Wow. That was super corny."

"I know. We're adorable. Now *tell me*."

"Fine. It's a potato gun."

"A *what*? That's a thing?"

"That's a thing. Homemade with black PVC pipe. See the lawn mower ignition connected to it? That's the real giveaway that he isn't just a student plumber with homework. That PVC pipe shoots potatoes like a cannon."

"You're telling me I found a rotting potato next to the crime scene, and the brother of one of the suspects owns a potato gun?

That's quite a coincidence."

"I'd say."

"How many of those can there be out there?"

"Potato guns? Millions."

"Really?"

"Okay, millions might be an exaggeration, but they're not that weird. Kids make them in high school and college."

"So you've built one of these before?"

He nodded, and she shook her head, baffled.

"Boy, men are even weirder than I thought."

He chuckled. "You have no idea. So do you think Bucky's girlfriend stole her brother's potato gun and shot him with it?"

Charlotte's lips twisted into a knot as she tried to picture Shawna using the PVC gun. "I don't know. She had access to him during his most unguarded moments. Why blast him off a roof? And a potato cannon doesn't really seem like your average girl's weapon of choice."

"I've heard that's poison."

"Speaking of which, do you want something to eat?"

"Nice timing. I'll pass. It's later than you think."

Charlotte looked at the clock on her stove and saw that it was nearly two in the morning. "Oh gosh. No wonder I'm exhausted. Arm wrestling, cow herding, blood bathing..."

Declan moved to stand, but she leaned on his shoulder, pushing him back into his seat.

"Wait, don't go yet. I'm thinking about Dallas."

"Texas?"

"No, Dallas is Shawna's brother's name. It's *his* potato gun."

She grabbed the thumb drive she'd found in Bucky's file and popped it back into her computer before sitting down. Flipping through video of people entering the marina building, she paused on a familiar couple.

Declan leaned to see the screen. "That's the video from Bucky's building?"

"Yes. And that's Bucky and Shawna," she said, pointing as two figures entered the building.

Not long after the couple disappeared, a man wearing a

black, hooded sweatshirt approached the door. She paused the screen and did her best to magnify the image.

"Does that look weird to you?" she said, pointing at the man's back.

Declan squinted at the blurry image. "It looks shaded there. Sort of square and cut-off?"

"It's hard to tell, but that's what I was thinking...like there is something covering his back."

The video was in black and white and not high resolution, but Charlotte could discern four light-colored half-circles sitting low on his sweatshirt. They appeared to be the lower half of a larger design that had been covered.

"I think he duct-taped over a logo."

Declan nodded and pointed to the same row of circular spots to which she'd been drawn. "What are these at the bottom?"

"I can't make it out. It's like four little bird faces with beaks?"

He grunted. "Maybe. I could see that. But it would be weird."

"*Think*. What would it be? A sports team logo, maybe? Why would he want to cover it up?"

Declan stretched his back and yawned. "Because it identifies him? Maybe it's from a place that he works?"

Charlotte jumped in her chair. "Yes. Or a place he goes to school." She switched to a browser and searched for Florida International University. When the logo appeared, they both gasped.

"A paw."

One version of the college logo had the initials of the school with a panther crawling forward from it. The outstretched paw had four toes, four circular toes with claws in the center of each, which looked very much like bird beaks.

"Shawna said Dallas goes to college at FIU. It has to be him."

"But he isn't carrying a potato gun."

"Isn't he?" She rewound the film, and they watched him appear in frame and open the door. He walked with a stiff, unnatural gait, his back to the camera. "He could be holding it against his body. We just can't see it from this camera angle."

"I guess—"

"Oh!" Charlotte yelped and pushed the laptop aside to dig through the police report papers until she retrieved a photo of Bucky on the slab.

"Round bruises," she said, pointing to Bucky's naked chest. "Think a potato bruise would look like this?"

Declan pressed his lips tight, nodding slowly. "I can only guess, mind you, since my high school buddies and I were careful *not* to shoot each other with potatoes, but yes."

"Could the force of one of those knock someone over a railing?"

"They could definitely get the process started. They're powerful."

"So I'm not crazy?"

"To think Bucky's mistress' brother killed him with a potato gun?"

"Yes."

"As crazy as that sounds, no. You certainly have enough to take it to the police and let them sort it out."

She grinned and then sobered.

"What is it?" asked Declan.

"Shawna. I wonder if she was in on it."

"Killing Bucky meant no more gifts for her."

"Unless she talked him into putting her in his will. Oh no..."

"What?"

"I think I have to call Stephanie."

Declan snarled much the way he had after smelling the potato and stood. "I'm afraid if you talk to her after midnight, she appears."

"You're right. It's too late. Maybe I should wait until tomorrow."

"Call her. She doesn't sleep. I bet you five bucks she doesn't even mention how late it is."

"Really?" Charlotte found her phone and dialed. She was about to hang up when Stephanie answered.

"If it isn't Miss Charlotte," said Stephanie.

"Hi. Sorry to bother you so late, but I have a quick question for you."

"You need tips on how to please Declan? I knew this call was coming. Is he there? I'll try and talk you through, keeping in mind your limited assets and skill set."

Charlotte took a deep breath and did her best to control her temper. If she made Stephanie angry, she wouldn't receive the answer to her question.

"No, thanks. It's about Bucky. Have you seen his will?"

"His will? What's that got to do with anything?"

Stephanie's voice grew sharp, and her demeanor changed, like a cat shifting from playing with a mouse to preparing to devour it.

"I'm following a lead, and I wanted to know if he left anything to anyone other than Cora."

"Why?"

Charlotte paused. She didn't want to say too much and give Stephanie the opportunity to share her findings with the competition. "I don't want to say, not yet, but it would be helpful."

Stephanie paused. "They're executing the will Monday. Cora will be at her lawyer's office. I can text you the information."

Charlotte was so taken aback by Stephanie's helpful demeanor that she found herself stunned into silence.

"Is that all?" asked Stephanie.

"Oh. Yes. Thank you."

"Thanks for redecorating my car, by the way. Don't think it went unnoticed."

For Charlotte, mirth and dread swirled in equal parts as Stephanie hung up.

"How'd that go?" asked Declan.

"Strangely well."

"Don't be fooled. She does that to keep us guessing."

"You're right. Now is when I should be most scared. But she says she's going to text me the information I need to find out if

Shawna is in Bucky's will."

"Good. At least it looks like you have a pretty strong case against Dallas."

Charlotte nodded in agreement and decided to keep her findings from the police for a little longer. First, she'd flesh out her theory as much as possible by confirming Shawna was in or out of Bucky's will, and then she'd present the police—and Cora—with everything she had.

Surely, solving Bucky's murder would win Penny her land.

But first, she needed to *sleep*.

CHAPTER TWENTY-THREE

The Day Bucky Died

Stephanie sat on the edge of the dock, eating popcorn and staring up at Bucky Bloom. Predictably, the old letch was enjoying his evening Scotch atop the marina apartments where he met with his Twinkie every Tuesday.

Soon they'd go out to dinner and *blah, blah, blah.*

Men are the worst.

Sure, she'd cheated on Declan during their romance, but that hadn't been about something as base as *sex*. That had been about *money*.

Entirely different.

She considered her history with Declan a moment longer and found she had to admit one caveat.

Her cheating on Declan had *mostly* been about money.

The Argentinean polo player had been a *little* bit about sex.

I'm only human.

Peering back at the roof, she knew she shouldn't complain about finding Bucky there. His predictability made him easy to tail and easier still to manipulate. Their time together was drawing to a close, though. The sooner she had Bucky's land for her mother, the sooner she could get back to her own life.

For now, she couldn't let Bucky out of her sight. That was the secret to her success. She left nothing to chance. She didn't assume Bucky would show up on time for Twinkie Tuesday—she watched Bucky *show up* for Twinkie Tuesday

Speaking of the Twinkie...

Shawna appeared on the roof beside Bucky, leaning over the railing, her arms thrust behind her, her long dark hair fluttering in the wind.

Re-enacting Titanic.

How original.

The girl disappeared, and Bucky returned to sipping his drink.

Stephanie was about to look away when Bucky suddenly spun, turning his back toward the railing. There was a muffled *boom!* and his torso flung back, weight shifting.

She clocked the moment he reached the point of no return. Unable to stop his momentum, Bucky flipped over the railing and began a rapid descent.

Stephanie traced his drop, the fall stopping abruptly fifty feet before he should have hit the docks below. Her jaw creaked open as Bucky, impaled on the mast of his own boat, twitched one last time and fell still.

That was insane.

She saw a flash of something black crouching below the wall where Bucky had been standing. She grabbed her binoculars and kept her gaze trained on the spot, but whatever she'd seen, it never resurfaced.

A crunching *bang!* echoed behind her, and she turned in time to watch a sailboat slam into one of the docks. The woman on the sailboat's bow uttered a yip of surprise and tumbled into the water. The flustered captain threw up his hands and panicked, slamming the boat into drive and then reverse several times.

Stephanie laughed.

Could this get any better?

She turned her attention to the door of the marina and remained riveted to it for nearly two hours, patiently watching every policeman enter and leave. It took them an hour to move the sailboat to the dockside club mast crane, remove the mast, and slide Bucky from it. The entire process was fascinating. It made it difficult to keep her attention focused on the door.

Once the police cleared the area and Bucky and Twinkie had been carted away, each in very different states of being, Stephanie spotted her prize exit the building.

"There you are, you little scamp," she mumbled.

Surprise, surprise.

She crumpled the popcorn bag in her hand and stood.

I have a lot to do.

Barely containing her grin, she headed for her car.

Things had gotten *much* more interesting.

CHAPTER TWENTY-FOUR

After Bucky's Fall

Stephanie followed the figure leaving the marina apartment building on foot and then by car. Tailing people was the only time she regretted owning a Dodge Viper. Fiery red sports vehicles didn't exactly *blend in.*

Her suspect's car didn't head where she'd expected. Instead, it pulled onto a very familiar road with only one large house on it.

Bucky's house.

The car stopped in front of Bucky's. The figure hopped out and ran to the front door as Stephanie watched from a distance.

Isn't this interesting.

Stephanie took a moment to think, running through every possible scenario. She wanted to make sure that once she knocked on that door, there were no surprises.

She turned off the Viper and made her way to Bucky's door.

A housekeeper answered.

"Nobody is home," she said before Stephanie could ask or state her business. In the background, she could hear a woman's voice, frantic.

She sighed and tilted her head to the side as if regarding a child.

"Really?"

Stephanie strode into the home with little resistance from the housekeeper. Following the sound of voices, she found herself in the living room, where an old woman and a young man huddled together in frozen silence as if their stillness rendered them invisible.

"I can see you, you know," said Stephanie.

"Who are you?" asked the woman.

From her surveillance of Bucky, Stephanie recognized her as his long-suffering wife, Cora Bloom.

She crossed her arms across her chest. "I think the better question is, who are *you*?"

"Who am I? I'm Cora Bloom. This is *my* house."

"No, I know you're Bucky's wife. I mean, *who are you*? I really didn't see this coming from you."

"What are you—"

Stephanie held up a palm. "Please. Let me do the talking. First, tell the maid to go. You're not going to want her to hear this."

Cora's gaze bounced past Stephanie, who turned to find the maid standing at the entry to the room.

"Go," said Cora.

"Are you sure, Miss Cora?"

"Yes. I'll be fine. Go."

The maid scowled and left through the front door. Stephanie stepped to the window and watched her enter her car and drive off before returning her attention to Cora.

The old woman's hands curled into fists by her sides. "If you don't get out of my house right now, I'm going to call the police."

Stephanie laughed and pointed to the young man. "Call the police? With him here? I don't think so. Not when I just watched him kill your husband."

The blood ran from Cora's face.

"You don't look surprised to hear Bucky is dead. I guess Dallas already told you?"

At the sound of his name, the boy, too, fell ashen and dropped his head into his hands. "I can't go to prison. I didn't mean it..."

Stephanie rolled her eyes. "It's a little late for blubbering. You should have thought about that before you attacked a wobbly old man standing near a precipice. What we need to do now is fix this."

The two snapped their attention to Stephanie, tears halting mid-stream.

"You're not going to turn me in?" asked Dallas.

"No. Why would I do that? Neither of you are any good to me in prison. No, I'm going to do this the old-fashioned way. Blackmail."

Dallas slapped his hand to his chest. "Me?"

Stephanie chuckled. "Uh, *no*, thanks. I'm full-up with jock straps and empty beer cans at the moment. I was thinking *her*."

Cora placed a hand on either cheek, and Stephanie chuckled. "Don't do that. You look like Edvard Munch's *The Scream*."

Cora dropped her hands to point at Dallas. "He wasn't supposed to kill him. He was only supposed to scare him. This isn't my fault."

"Are you sure a jury would see it that way after they realize your filthy rich husband was killed moments after diddling his young mistress?"

Cora huffed. "I've put up with that for years. Why would I kill him now?"

"I don't know. Mine is not to question why. Mine is but to *stand as witness and tell them I saw anything I damn well please*."

Dallas whimpered again, and Stephanie trained her focus on him. "Let's take care of you first. Where's the weapon?"

He peered at her through teary eyes. "The weapon?"

"Bucky's body jerked before he fell. You shot him?"

"Kinda."

"How do you kinda shoot someone?"

"I had a potato gun."

Stephanie paused, her mouth still open. "You shot him with a *what*?"

"A potato gun. I brought it back from college. It's PVC pipe, and then you fill the back of it with something, like, really flammable. My buddy's mom had a beauty salon, and he got his hands on, like, three cases of old-school AquaNet hairspray, so we used that. Then you stuff a potato down the throat, and we've got this outdoor grill ignition that sets off the hairspray, and *boom!*"

Dallas threw out his hands to simulate the force of the projectile.

"So it's powerful?"

"Oh yeah. You could knock someone's head off with one of those things—" Dallas realized what he had said and tried to backtrack. "But, I mean, I didn't load it with much, and I was aiming at his stomach..."

Stephanie winked at Cora. "Boy, he'd be great on the stand, wouldn't he, Cora? Want to put your life in Dallas' hands? Feeling secure?"

Dallas moaned. "I swear it was an *accident*. I'll tell the judge that she told me to scare him, not kill him. The gun jerked, and I hit him higher than I meant to, and he tipped—"

Stephanie offered him a condescending smile. "Dallas, sweetheart, I'm a criminal attorney. What if I told you that if you agreed to state on the record that Cora *demanded* you kill Bucky, you could walk away scot-free? Would your story change?"

Dallas' mouth hung open, eyes darting to Cora.

Cora's eyes flashed with fear. "But I never said that. He came to *me* because he didn't want Bucky dating his sister, and he knew I didn't either. He offered to scare him away."

"He offered to scare him away for free?"

Cora and Dallas exchanged a glance.

Stephanie nodded. "That's what I thought. You gave him money. I don't suppose that money is already in your bank account?"

Dallas shook his head. "It's at home. I can give it back..."

"Check?"

"Cash," said Cora. "I'm not stupid," she added, muttering.

"No paper trail. Excellent. Congratulations to you both on

entering the lucrative field of kill-for-hire."

Dallas threw back his head so it bounced on the sofa. "But she didn't pay me to kill—"

Stephanie shook her head. "Stop. We're past that. Let's see, the long and the short of it is that you knocked Bucky over the wall with a potato gun. I guess, on the upside, we don't have to worry about ballistics. Where'd you dump it?"

"What?"

"The gun. The potato."

"I picked up the potato chunks, broke up the gun, and put it in the trash."

"What trash?"

"The trash in the men's bathroom in the lobby of the first floor."

"Great, black PVC pipe won't look suspicious mixed in with the paper towels."

Dallas scowled. "You said that kinda funny."

"It's called *sarcasm*. Did you at least wipe your fingerprints off it?"

If it was possible, Dallas grew even paler. "No. Dammit. I shouldn't have thrown it out...that was so stupid. I was just so afraid to leave the building with it."

"Okay. I'm done with you for now. Go home."

"What? But—"

Stephanie flashed him her most serious glare. "*Go home.* Don't ever go back to the marina and don't come back here, understand? I don't want you *ever* talking to Cora again. Keep your money and go back to school. Did she give you enough?"

"For the semester—"

"How much to finish school entirely?"

"I only have a year left, so...like...seven thousand with books and everything?"

"Hm. How much cash do you have in the house, Cora?"

"What? I—"

"You know what, never mind. I'll tack it on to my fee, and I'll get him the cash."

"Your fee?" asked Cora.

"We'll get to that in a minute. Now, Dallas, do we have a deal? You get enough money to finish college, I clean up your mess, and you never see Cora or the marina or anything that has to do with Bucky again. You never mention what happened. It's like it never did. Deal?"

Dallas seemed stunned into silence.

"Let me add that the alternative is that I turn you in, hand the potato gun over to the police, and you spend the rest of your life in jail."

Dallas stood. "I'm good. I'll never say a word. I promise."

"One other thing. Does your sister know?"

"No."

"Good. She never finds out either."

"No. She's the last person I'd tell."

"Right. Now get out of here."

Dallas mumbled thanks and bolted from the room.

"Now, Cora. Let's sit a spell."

Stephanie sat on the sofa where Dallas had been, and Cora lowered herself into her chair.

"What do you want from me?"

Stephanie grinned. "I'll let you know after they execute the will. Until then, you and I are going to become fast friends."

CHAPTER TWENTY-FIVE

Sunday, nearly a week after Bucky's fall and a day after the Cow Town challenge…

"You're skulking around me like the shadow of death—how long are you going to keep me trapped like this?" asked Cora.

Stephanie cocked her head and stared at her shoe as she bobbed it up and down on her toe. "Maybe I just like your company."

In truth, she was as sick of Cora as the woman was of her, but she had no choice but to keep an eye on her. Nothing could go wrong, and only Cora had the ability to stop her.

Cora fidgeted. "You're watching me like a hawk, and I don't know why. It makes me very nervous."

"What *should* make you nervous is knowing that if you upset me, I'll have you put in jail for colluding to kill your husband before the dirt settles on Bucky's coffin."

Cora looked away, wringing her hands.

Stephanie sighed. "I'm sorry. That was cruel and unnecessary."

Cora scoffed. "What's cruel and unnecessary is inviting yourself to my weekly bridge game and telling all my friends that I'm a terrible player."

"You are. Awful. But you're right, that was rude. Forgive me?"

Cora whipped her head toward Stephanie like a mongoose. "Do I have a choice?"

Stephanie raised her arms. "There we go. There's some of the old fire back. I think if you give it a moment's thought, you'll realize you're not approaching our time together with the right *attitude*. Can't you get into the spirit? After all, the competition between Penny and Tabby is fun, isn't it? That was your idea."

"It was *not* my idea."

"Now, that's not true. I was in the kitchen when those women appeared, sniffing around for Cow Town, pretending to care about Bucky's death. You were livid. You even forgot about me for a minute, didn't you?"

"It was hard to forget you, what with you lurking in the kitchen—"

"But you *did* forget about me. Just for a second."

Cora sniffed. "Maybe. They were just so *transparent*—"

"Exactly. And you were *mad*. Admit it."

"I was. Though, I might have been taking other aggressions out on them."

"You mean *me* and our little situation. I understand. It won't be much longer. I promise. But in the meantime, let's have some fun. What else do you want from them? One more contest for old times' sake?"

Cora's hand fluttered to her forehead, and she tucked away an errant strand of hair. "I don't want anything from those two harpies."

"Come on. How else are you going to decide who to sell the land to? You told them *figure it out*, and now you have to show them *how*. The landscaping idea really showed that Tabby was the more repentant of the two, don't you think? That was brilliant."

"Telling them I lost my landscaping man was your idea."

"Exactly. Like I said, brilliant. Now, what else do you need?"

"I don't need anything."

"What about arrangements for the funeral?"

"I'm not going to ask those Jezebels to help with my husband's funeral."

"Mm. I guess not. How about something for someone else? Don't you have grandkids?"

"Of course, I've told you all about them."

"Oh, right, how could I forget—"

Cora beamed and cut her short. "It's my granddaughter Lily's fourth birthday next week. But I don't see what that has to do with anything."

"Fourth birthday. What did you get her?"

"For a present? I—" Cora's expression fell. "Oh my. With Bucky's death...I totally forgot."

"There you go. That's our answer. Let the ladies compete to find a birthday gift for Lulu."

"*Lily*. But they don't even *know* my granddaughter."

"Who needs to know her? She's four. She's a little psychopath in pullup pants like every other four-year-old on the planet. And like you said, let *them* figure it out."

"I guess if it would make you happy and bring an end to this nonsense."

"It would. That's the spirit. I'm going to go out for a bit. You stay here. You know what happens if you don't do as I say."

Cora rolled her eyes. "I know, I know."

Stephanie waved to the ever-present housekeeper, who all but growled at her, and walked to her car. Driving back to her office to catch up on work, she passed a strip mall and noticed a specialty toy shop next to the Publix called Buy Their Love: Toys and Unique Gifts. She'd never noticed it before, but now, it was as if a spotlight was shining down on it.

She pulled into the parking lot and walked into the shop, where she was greeted by a wall of tan Teddy bears.

"Hello?"

No answer.

The place appeared empty of both customers and staff. She strolled the aisles, searching for signs of life.

A woman stepped from the back of the store and jumped

upon seeing her.

"Oh. You scared me. I didn't hear you come in. Can I help you?"

Stephanie scanned the shelf in front of her and realized she knew nothing about four-year-olds or their tastes in toys. "Yes, I could use some help. What would you suggest for a four-year-old?"

"Boy or girl?"

"Girl."

The woman thought for a moment and then led Stephanie to another aisle. "Anything in this area would work."

Stephanie's gaze swept over the collection of pink packaged delights, and she grunted with dissatisfaction.

"This all seems so gender-biased."

"What?"

"Do you have anything less *pink*?"

"Oh, of course. You know, we don't sell the same things you can find just anywhere. We specialize in unique, high-quality items."

"What about those teddy bears at the front of the store? Are they unique?"

The woman glowed with pride. "Oh, they're *very* special. Imported from Germany. They're Steiff. They invented the Teddy bear in nineteen oh-two."

Stephanie frowned. "Really? I thought Morris Michtom, from Brooklyn, New York made the first Teddy bears in nineteen oh-two after the news ran stories about Teddy Roosevelt refusing to kill a captive bear?"

The woman's mouth fell open. "I, I don't know. I never heard that story. Where did you hear that?"

"Who knows?" Stephanie shrugged and tapped her temple with her finger as she walked back to the bears. She took a step back from their display shelves and surveyed them.

"How many are there here, do you think?"

The woman began to point and count out loud. Stephanie cut her off.

"I'll save you the trouble. Eighteen. Do you have any more

in the back?"

"More? No."

"What time do you close?

"Five."

Stephanie looked at her watch. It was four-thirty.

"Tell you what. I'll buy all the bears except one, and I'll have a friend of mine come and pick up that last bear before you close. But there's a catch: you have to promise me you won't sell that last bear to anyone except him."

"Why would you want all of the bears?"

Stephanie arched an eyebrow. "Do you want to ask me questions, or do you want to sell eighteen bears?"

"Oh, the bears. The bears." The woman jogged behind the register.

Stephanie set her credit card on the counter. "Do you have a trash bag or something I could put them in?"

The woman dipped behind the counter and reappeared with a plastic trash bag in her hand.

Stephanie took it and began filling it with bears. "This place is a ghost town. How do you stay in business?"

"What's that? Did you say how do I stay in business?"

Stephanie motioned for a second bag, and the woman handed one to her. "Yes. It's been forever since I've seen a small, privately-owned toy store. What with the Internet..."

The woman nodded as she ran Stephanie's card. "*Oh*, yes. That's true. It helps that the residents in the area are older. Many of them don't trust the Internet and like to shop the old-fashioned way."

"Makes sense."

The woman handed Stephanie her receipt and a business card. Stephanie was about to stuff it in her pocket when something on it caught her eye.

"You have a website?"

The woman laughed. "Oh yes. We'd go out of business without it."

Stephanie nodded and hoisted the bag of bears over her shoulder like a very single-minded Santa before heading back to her car.

CHAPTER TWENTY-SIX

Seamus sat in the cool, air-conditioned bliss of The Striped Goldfish, a hole-in-the-wall bar he'd come to appreciate. The Guinness beer wasn't as fresh as in Ireland—where keeping a Guinness tap primed and flowing was akin to a religion—but he'd had worse. As a matter of coincidence, Billy, the owner of the Goldfish, had Irish forbears and possessed massive pride in the state of his Irish beer.

"How ya doin' today, Seamus?" asked Billy, proceeding to pour Seamus a pint without waiting for a request.

"It's been an odd week, Billy. I can tell you that much."

"Sounds like you need a beer."

"You're a gentleman and a genius." Billy set down the beer, and Seamus lifted his pint in salute.

Billy leaned on the bar and stared at Seamus' face as he took his first quaff, which Seamus would have found unnerving if it didn't happen every time he stopped at the Goldfish. Billy always wanted to know if the Guinness lager was as fresh as it could be.

"How is it?" asked Billy.

"As good as it can get this far from Ireland. You've done it again."

Billy flashed his gap-toothed grin. "Means a lot coming from you."

"I know. I won't let you slip."

Seamus heard the creak of the bar's front door followed by a man's voice.

"*Dios mio.*"

He turned to find Edmundo had entered the pub. Making a quick circle in the sky with his index finger, he returned his attention to his beer. "Just turn right around and head back the way you came, Eddie."

Eddie chuckled and sat at the end of the bar, facing Seamus. "I should have known. The peeling paint, the darkened windows; this place had you written all over it."

Billy approached him for an order.

"I'll take a Cuba libre."

Billy chuckled and flashed Seamus a look. "Should I charge him extra for using such fancy words to order a rum and Coke?"

"Whatever you charge him, watch him closely. He's a crafty bugger."

"I am. See here. Get me a shot of whiskey and a shot of water."

"A rum and coke, a shot, and a water?" asked Billy.

"Hear me out. I will make you a wager. If I can put the whiskey into the glass that holds the water, and the water into the glass that holds the whiskey, without putting either into a third container, the shot is free."

Billy scowled as he poured the whiskey. "You're saying you'll switch what is in each glass without using a third glass?"

"Yes."

"And you don't mean mixed up…each to each?"

"Yes."

Billy glanced at Seamus, who shook his head. "I wouldn't do it."

Billy thought for a moment and then shrugged. "Nah, I'd like to see this." He sat one shot glass of whiskey and one with an equal amount of water in front of Eddie.

Eddie shook his head. "They have to be full. To the very top, not the line. You don't want me to do half a job, do you?"

Billy shrugged and topped each glass off.

"There you go."

Eddie retrieved his wallet from his back pocket and pulled a business card from it. He sat it on top of the water glass. He snapped out his arms like a magician preparing to perform a trick. "Ready?"

Billy waved his arms. "Wait, wait, I think I figured this out. You're going to put one in your mouth. You said you couldn't use another *glass,* but you'll use your mouth."

"No, I will not use my mouth, I promise."

Billy grunted.

Eddie wiggled his fingers again and then rested his hands on the bar. "You know, this is too hard. I don't think I can even attempt it unless my Cuba libre is free as well."

"You want the shot and the drink for free if you do it?"

"I think that is only fair."

"And you're not going to use anything to transfer them? Not a glass, not your mouth—"

"No."

"Then fine, yeah, I'll give you the rum and Coke on the house, too." He said, grabbing a bottle of rum to make it.

"Oh, Billy," muttered Seamus, dropping his head to rest on his arms on the bar.

Billy turned to him. "What? It's impossible."

Eddie winked at Seamus, who shook his head.

"Okay, here I go." Eddie held the business card tight to the top of the water shot glass and flipped it over, sitting it neatly on top of the whiskey glass. Only the business card and the weight of the shot glass full of water kept the water from spilling out.

Billy chuckled. "That's kind of cool, but it didn't win you any free drinks."

"Ah, but I'm not done."

Eddie slid the business card from the glasses by a fraction of an inch, opening a gap between the upper and lower liquids. The glass of water began to grow golden as a thread of whiskey rose into it like a genie from a bottle.

"What the—how are you doing that?"

"Water is heavier than whiskey," said Seamus.

"So?"

"So eventually, all the water will be in the bottom glass, and the whiskey will be up top."

Billy grimaced and shook his head. "That's not right."

Eddie took a sip of his Cuba libre and grinned.

"Didn't I warn you?" Seamus asked Billy.

"How was I supposed to know how much water weighs?"

Seamus scowled. "First off, it's a bar trick. Everyone who's spent a lot of time in a bar knows it."

"I own a bar."

"For how long?"

"Six months."

"And before that, did you spend a lot of time in bars?"

Billy's gaze dropped to the ground. "Wife wouldn't let me. But it was always my dream to own one."

"There you go. Second—and this is the most important thing to remember, the thing that will save you, even if you can't remember all the tricks—if a relatively sober person in a bar ever says, 'I bet you I can,' no matter how crazy it sounds, *don't bet them*. They *can*."

Billy pointed at him. "Oh yeah? I heard about a guy in a bar who bet everyone he could fly, and he fell to his death."

"I said anyone *relatively sober*. That is an important distinction."

Billy peered at the glasses. The liquids had nearly completed their switch. "I still think he cheated."

Seamus sighed. "See, Billy, now I have to reclaim your honor for you."

Billy grumbled, *reclaim this,* and wandered to the back.

"How do you propose to avenge your friend?" asked Eddie.

Seamus smiled. "Doesn't this place remind you of anything?"

"Hell?"

"Come on." Seamus nodded toward the pool table in the back of the room and then toward the dart board on the far wall.

Eddie shook his head. "Oh no. Forget it. You're a terrible loser. The last time we played, you threw a dart in my thigh."

"That was an accident, and you know it. You whacked me in the small of my back with your pool cue."

"Because you threw a dart at me."

"It happened in that order?"

"Yes."

Seamus grunted. "Mm. That does sound like me."

The two men stared at each other in silence until Eddie released a long, labored sigh. "Fine. You win. Let's play."

Seamus drained the last of his beer and stood. "Pool first."

An hour later, the two men sat side by side, poking wildly at a bar-top arcade machine, searching for a game to act as a tiebreaker. Eddie had won best of three at pool, and Seamus had taken darts.

Seamus' phone chirped, and he ignored it. Eddie fished in his pocket for his phone.

"It was my phone," said Seamus, trying to navigate the endless menu of games on the video screen.

Eddie glanced at his screen and then slipped his phone back into his pocket.

"You know, I have some cards out in the car. We can settle this like men."

"Yeah?"

"Yeah. I don't like these video games. There is no honor in them. I'll get the cards."

"Sounds like a plan."

Eddie stood and left.

Time passed until Seamus found himself glancing at the door for the tenth time and still found no sign of Eddie's return.

"How long ago did he leave?" he asked Billy, who stood with a newspaper in front of his face.

Billy shrugged. "Maybe five minutes?"

"Think it takes that long to get a pack of cards out of a car?"

"Depends on where the car is and where the cards are, but I'd say no."

"Shite."

"What's the matter? Spill your beer?" asked Billy, glancing out from behind his news.

"He pulled a runner. Left me with the tab."

Billy pointed at Seamus. "Ha. So I'm not the only one falling for his tricks."

Seamus slid from his stool and jogged to the door. His car was the only vehicle in the lot.

He cursed liberally.

"I'm going to kill that—"

Seamus froze, remembering the sound of his phone dinging.

Eddie had looked at *his* phone right before he left.

Seamus fumbled his phone from his pocket and spotted a text from Stephanie.

Cora needs a teddy bear for her granddaughter's niece. Today. Store closes at five.

He looked at the time on his phone. It was four forty.

"Bastard."

Jerking money from his wallet, he slapped it on the bar before bolting for the door.

"This isn't near enough," called Billy.

"We'll settle up later."

Seamus ran to his car and roared out of the parking lot.

CHAPTER TWENTY-SEVEN

"Teddy bear, Teddy bear, Teddy bear," Seamus chanted, heading for the shopping district.

He cursed again and fumbled to dial his phone.

Charlotte answered.

"Hey, Seamus—"

"Shut it, no time."

"Okaaay..."

"Did you get a text from Stephanie?"

"No. Did you?"

"She wants me to get a Teddy bear."

"Any Teddy bear?"

"Yes. I think so. Do you know where?"

"No, *where*?"

"No, I'm asking *you* where. Where can I get one? She said the shop closes at five. I've got fifteen minutes to figure it out and buy it, and Eddie has a five-minute head start on me."

"Eddie? How does—"

"*Where* do they sell Teddy bears?

"Oh, um...shop closes at five, so it isn't one of the big chain stores...oh. There's a toy shop in the same plaza as the Publix. Buy Their Love. It's got to be there."

"Good. Great."

Seamus hung up and hit the gas to slip through a yellow light.

Peeling into the Publix parking lot, he spotted the toy shop.

Eddie's unmistakable car sat in the lot adjacent to the store.

Seamus pointed his clunker toward the first available parking spot as Eddie stepped out of his car and started toward the shop.

Gritting his teeth, Seamus swerved away from the slot he'd been eying and screeched around the parked cars to pull to the curb in front of the toy shop. His car impeded his foe's progress so abruptly that Eddie had to jump back to avoid being hit. His face flashed with anger.

The men locked gazes, and Eddie pointed at his nemesis.

"No."

Eddie lunged to dodge around the front of the car. Seamus hit the gas, blocking him. Eddie slapped the hood with both hands and bolted for the back of the car. Seamus shifted into reverse, but when he looked up, he saw Eddie had reversed himself and now bolted past the *front* of his car.

"He juked me."

Seamus threw the car into park and scrambled out the passenger side. He lunged for the door of the shop as Eddie opened it and managed to get half his body into the store before Eddie realized what was happening and pushed the door shut, pinching him like a mouse in a trap.

"Hey!" yelped Seamus, the arm that hadn't made it into the store, flailing in an attempt to grab Eddie.

The woman behind the counter in the toy store stared at him, frozen with what looked like something between confusion and fear.

"That bear..." he pointed at the only Teddy bear sitting on the large empty shelves inside the shop. "I want that bear."

"I want the bear," demanded Eddie, leaning his full weight on the door in an attempt to keep Seamus pinned.

"I'm holding it for someone," said the woman.

Seamus grunted, worried his ribs might break.

"Me. You're holding him for me—"

Seamus reached for his wallet with the hand inside the store, only to realize it was in his opposite pocket. He ceased slapping at Eddie and snatched his wallet with his right hand. Lifting, he tried to pass the wallet from his outside hand to his inside hand over his head. Eddie noticed and slapped his arm. The wallet flew, spinning to the cement.

"Hey!"

Eddie eased his pressure against the door, grabbed Seamus' right arm with both hands, and attempted to jerk him from the store.

Losing what little ground he'd made, Seamus tried to make his case with the cashier, his words escaping in staccato bursts between each tug.

"You're—holding—the—bear—*shite! Stop it, you Ricky Ricardo mother*—for—me!"

The woman curled her hands into fists of frustration. "Prove it. What's the name of the woman who bought the rest of them?"

"Stephanie!" called Eddie as he tried to pry Seamus' fingers off the door frame.

Seamus tried to out-shout him. "I knew that. It's Stephanie."

With one last mighty jerk, Eddie dislodged Seamus from the door and spun him toward the curb. The Miami detective skittered inside, reaching for the bear.

Seamus caught his balance and scooped up his wallet as he lunged for the door.

Eddie grabbed the bear, but before he could turn to the counter, Seamus opened the door and leapt at him like a tiger, tackling him to the ground.

They hit the ground with a great expelling of air. The two of them wrestled with the bear until they heard the sound of tearing fabric. A flurry of polyester fibers exploded in the air around them.

They froze.

With a dejected shrug, Eddie rolled on his back, arms splayed. "I am too old for this."

Seamus propped himself against a shelf of wooden cars, panting. He glanced at his lap. Plastic eyes stared back at him from a bear's severed head.

With an abundance of grunting and groaning, he climbed to his feet and walked toward the door, the head in his hands.

"Someone has to pay for that," said the woman.

"He's got it," said Seamus.

Outside, he brushed the stuffing from his shirt and slipped into his car.

He dialed Charlotte.

"Good news, bad news."

"You didn't get it?"

"That's the bad news."

"Then what's the good news?"

"He didn't get it either."

"The store was closed?"

"Sure, let's say—" He sputtered and pulled stuffing from his lips. "Let's say that."

"So you think this one will be a tie?"

He turned the ignition and tossed the bear head into his passenger seat. "I don't know. We might be a little ahead."

CHAPTER TWENTY-EIGHT

Monday afternoon, Charlotte headed into the office building of Cora's lawyer, hoping that the reading of the will would prove whether Shawna was involved or if her brother had acted alone. She didn't want the girl to be involved—she'd sounded sweet on the phone—but on the other hand, if Shawna was in Bucky's will, it would strengthen the validity of her potato gun murder theory.

She needed points either way. Penny had lost the landscape and arm-wrestling challenges. Only the cow challenge put them on the board. Their chance to tie, the Teddy bear challenge, had been a bust, literally.

She slipped into a closing elevator before noticing Cora Bloom inside, tucked in the corner.

"You're Penny's orphan," said Cora.

"Uh, yes. Sort of."

"What are you doing here?"

"I came to hear the reading of Bucky's will with your permission."

"Why?"

"Because I think it might hold a missing piece to your husband's death."

"Missing piece? What are you talking about? He fell. The only missing piece is that mast."

Charlotte grimaced. "I didn't want to tell you this way,

but…" She paused, unsure if she should continue.

"What? Tell me."

"I think your husband was murdered."

No sooner had she finished her sentence than Cora's eyes rolled back, and she crumpled forward.

"Cora!" Charlotte lunged forward and caught the diminutive woman. The elevator stopped, and the doors opened, so she dragged her to a bench in the hall and propped her on it. Running back, she stopped the doors from closing, snatched Cora's fallen purse from the ground, and returned to her patient.

She hovered over Cora's body. Eyes closed, Cora lay still, but for her breathing.

Not dead. Passed out.

Charlotte knew what people in movies did when confronted with an unconscious person, but slapping an old woman across the face didn't seem *right.*

"Cora…" She tapped the woman's wrinkled cheek lightly with all four fingers, effecting a slow-motion slap.

Nothing.

She stood and called out. "Hello? Can anyone hear me?" The closed doors at either end of the hallway remained shut.

She was about to dial 911 when Cora's eyes fluttered open.

"Cora, are you okay?"

Cora swallowed and sat up, seeming woozy.

"Yes. I'm fine." She took a moment to focus on Charlotte. "Did you say you think my husband was murdered?"

Charlotte paused, worried that talking about Bucky would send the woman swooning again. "Maybe we shouldn't talk about this now?"

"No. Tell me."

"Okay. I *do* have a theory that Bucky was murdered. It's a little crazy, but it is strangely plausible, if not likely."

"Have you told the police?"

"No, not yet. I wanted to hear the will first and talk to you."

Cora opened her purse and retrieved a handkerchief, which she dabbed against her head and lips. "What's your theory?"

"Do you want me to get into it now? Shouldn't we go—"

Cora's bony claw shot forward, and she grabbed Charlotte's shirt. "Tell me *now*."

Charlotte jumped, startled, and then eased back to pull her shirt from Cora's grasp. The woman let her hand fall into her lap.

"It's going to sound crazy," cautioned Charlotte once more.

Cora's eyes narrowed. "I don't *care*."

"Fine. I think I've found evidence that proves your husband was shot with a potato gun by Shawna's brother, Dallas."

Cora's expression didn't change but for the twitch of her cheek. She remained frozen, staring at Charlotte.

"Cora? Are you okay?"

"A potato gun? How could you know, *think*, that?" she whispered.

"I know it's *crazy*. I don't expect you to believe me right now, and I'm sure it's a lot to take in. I'm so sorry to be the one to tell you. Please keep in mind that this is a theory that came up during my investigation. It isn't iron-clad..."

Cora's brows knit. "Your investigation? Why were you investigating my husband's death?"

"To win for Penny. Remember? I was the one there with her when we came to see you with flowers—"

Cora's voice grew high and strained as she cut Charlotte short. "Why would you think proving that my husband's death was a murder would win you Cow Town?"

Because you said it was the most important task of all?"

"*I* did?"

"Yes—

"I did no such thing."

"But—"

Charlotte stopped and recalled how the directive to solve Bucky's murder had first come to her.

Oh right. Of course.

She said the name aloud.

"Stephanie."

"Are you working with her?" asked Cora, jerking to her feet

as if a rat had run across her lap.

"Working with her? No. I mean, only in the sense that she assigned us the tasks to win Cow Town. She said the group that could prove Bucky's death was murder, or *not* murder, would be the group that won."

"Why would she say that?"

"It wasn't your idea?"

Cora shook her head.

"She told me she'd help me make the sisters compete for the land, but she *never* said anything about asking you to solve Bucky's murder." Cora grew pale, and her gaze floated back to Charlotte. "And now you have?"

Charlotte shook her head. "I don't know that I have. Like I said, it's just a theory. If you didn't even know we were looking into the deaths...oh, Cora, I'm so sorry. This must come as a terrible shock. No wonder..." She wiggled her finger in the direction of the elevator. "I'm so sorry."

Cora took a deep breath and straightened her dress, nodding slowly. "Of course."

"It might be nice to know the truth, even if it is terrible, don't you think?" suggested Charlotte.

Cora patted Charlotte's hand. "Of course. Thank you."

"Do you want me to call you a doctor?"

"No, no. I'm fine. Let's go in."

Charlotte walked bedside Cora to her lawyer's office.

After a brief wait flipping through some shockingly boring magazines and a round of introductions, the lawyer read the will to the only two people present.

The outcome was short and to the point. Cora received everything.

"Is that what you expected to hear?" Cora asked.

Charlotte smiled. "It's what I hoped to hear. If Shawna had been added to Bucky's will, it would have meant she was almost certainly working with her brother. Since that didn't happen, it's looking more like Dallas just didn't like Bucky dating his sister."

She realized to whom she was talking and covered her

mouth. "Oh, sorry. I didn't mean to be indelicate."

Cora chuckled. "The days of Bucky's indiscretions shocking me are long past. But you had nothing to fear. Bucky loved his dalliances, but he never would have put one of those tramps in his will."

Cora thanked the lawyer. "Can you do me a favor, Bob? I need to transfer the deed to the lot by my house over to someone. Can you draw up the papers for that?"

The lawyer scowled. "Cow Town?"

She nodded.

"But, you don't have Cow Town."

Cora blinked. "What's that?"

"You don't own it anymore."

"You said he gave everything to me, didn't you?"

"Yes. But Bucky sold the Cow Town lot several weeks ago. Sale became final today."

"*What*?" said Cora and Charlotte together.

"Who? Who would he sell it to?" asked Cora.

"Um, I have that name here..." The lawyer rifled through the papers on his desk. "Here it is, a Ms. Moriarty. Seems he sold it to her quite reasonably, too."

Cora sputtered.

"*Stephanie* Moriarty?" asked Charlotte.

He nodded.

Charlotte touched Cora's arm. "Did you know?"

Instead of answering, Cora turned an evil glare on her lawyer. "Why didn't you tell me?"

The lawyer shook his head, his eyes wide with confusion. "I called once or twice to see if you wanted to come in and review everything before it was final, but I never heard back."

"You called? *Me*?"

"I called your cell. I have the number here..."

Cora retrieved her phone from her purse. "What number do you have?"

He read off the digits, and Cora nodded. "That's right, but I don't have any calls from you."

"Let me see," said Charlotte.

Cora handed her the phone, and Charlotte flipped through the settings.

"It's blocked."

"What?"

"His number is blocked. You might have thought it was a spam call, maybe, and blocked it?"

An expression of realization passed across Cora's face, and her shoulders relaxed. She slipped the phone from Charlotte's hand and dropped it back into her purse. "That's it. I must have. Thank you, Charlotte."

"There still might be time to stop the sale. You could fight it?"

Cora shook her head. "No, no. It's fine. I was going to sell it anyway. This is more off my plate. This is good. Thank you, Bob."

Cora wandered out of the room.

Charlotte looked at the lawyer, and he chuckled. "I thought she was going to kill me there for a second."

Charlotte sighed. "So did I."

CHAPTER TWENTY-NINE

"What are you doing here?" asked Darla.

"Taking the day off to celebrate solving the case," said Declan, pulling the towel from his shoulder and handing it to Charlotte as she stepped from the pool.

Charlotte smiled as he mentioned her dubious victory. She'd solved Bucky's murder but failed Penny. Worse still, Stephanie had once again found a way to disrupt her life.

"I don't know how much of a victory it is. Poor Cora had no idea how Bucky really died. She fainted when I told her I thought it was murder."

"I can only imagine. That *must* have been a shock," said Mariska, who sat next to Darla, drying from her own swim.

Declan chuckled. "There are a lot of broken hearts going around today. I opened the store for Blade this morning, and he was mourning the loss of his cat."

"He finally gave Johnnie Walker Cat back to Mr. French? Good. Poor Mr. French has been through enough this week, too," said Charlotte.

The gate squeaked, and they turned to find Frank, in full sheriff's uniform, entering the pool area.

"Little early for lunch, isn't it?" asked Darla.

"It's never too early for lunch, but that's not why I'm here. Charlotte, Tampa wants to know where you got that thumb drive."

"What thumb drive?"

"When I gave them back the Bucky envelope and told them about your theory, they said the video evidence of Dallas entering the building wasn't from them."

"Wasn't from them? But it was in the manila envelope you gave me."

"They say it wasn't. They said the footage from that camera had been destroyed when they looked for it."

Charlotte found herself speechless. "I don't know what to tell you. I found the thumb drive there...*oh*. Wait a second..." She recalled the mysterious ring from her video doorbell and the question mark on her chalkboard. She'd noticed the thumb drive after that, and *had* been surprised she hadn't noticed it earlier.

"Someone broke into my house."

Frank scowled. "Broke into your house? Why didn't you tell me?"

"Other than drawing a question mark on my chalkboard, I couldn't find that they'd done or taken anything. But now I'm thinking maybe they *left* something."

"The video? Why would someone do that?"

"Because they wanted to help me catch Dallas?"

Frank scoffed. "Well, a lot of good it did."

"What's that mean?"

"They can't find him. His sister said he went back to school, but his roommate says he never showed up at the apartment. He never showed up for any of his classes."

"He's on the run?"

"That would be my guess."

"That confirms he was guilty, right? Why else would he run?" asked Declan.

Charlotte nodded. "I guess."

"But what about someone breaking into Charlotte's house?" asked Darla.

Frank shrugged. "I guess if someone wanted Dallas caught, we should thank them for giving her the piece she needed."

Darla huffed. "You can't go breaking into people's houses—"

"It's a little convenient, don't you think?" asked Charlotte, thinking aloud.

"What do you mean?" asked Declan.

"Did someone want the guilty person caught? Or were they framing him?"

Frank laughed. "Stop second-guessing yourself. You did a great job. Armed with your theory, they showed Dallas' picture to some of Bucky's staff, and his assistant said she'd seen him before, yelling at Bucky to stay away from his sister."

Charlotte perked. "Really? I guess that makes me feel better..."

Frank patted her on the shoulder. "You found potato. He had a potato gun. What more do you need?"

Charlotte sighed. "I guess. Something just feels fishy."

Declan threw his arm around her and pulled her to him. "You always think that. And hey, now you should have enough official hours to get your investigator's license."

She beamed. "You're right."

"We'll have to have a party," said Mariska.

"Fine, but wait until I actually have it, if you would. I don't want to jinx it."

Charlotte heard her phone ring and reached into her pool bag to retrieve it.

"It's Stephanie," she said.

Declan shook his head. "Don't answer it."

She turned from the group and put the phone to her ear.

"Hello?"

"Still want the property?" asked Stephanie.

"Penny does, I'm sure."

"It's for sale. Tell her to submit her bid."

"For sale? Already?"

"Yes. If you have a problem with that—"

"No, not at all. It's just that there have been trucks and noise over there night and day. I assumed you were building something."

"Did you look up the building permits?"

Charlotte sighed. She hated to admit to Stephanie that she *had* cared enough to look for a permit. She'd found little.

"I only found permits for the fences you put up to keep us from seeing what was happening."

"You did look. I'm so impressed, really."

Charlotte rolled her eyes. "Stop. You're making me feel all warm and fuzzy inside."

"Did you peek too? Did you look inside the fence?"

"You were digging a foundation when I looked."

Stephanie laughed. "Submit your bid."

"I'll let Penny know."

She hung up, and Charlotte turned back to the group.

"What did she want?" asked Declan.

"To tell me Cow Town is for sale again. She wants Penny to bid."

"Already? Why did she even buy it?"

"I don't know. But I need to go take a peek at it. Want to come?"

Declan nodded, and they excused themselves. They took Charlotte's golf cart to the thin strip of brush that separated the Cow Town lot from Pineapple Port and picked their way through.

Standing against the pasture fence, they stood, jaws hanging slack, staring at a giant hole in the ground.

Grass, cow patties, and six feet of dirt had disappeared from a large portion of the field. It was as if someone had built a giant basement and then decided to abandon the house.

"Why would she do this?" asked Charlotte.

Declan leaned forward and peered into the hole. "Is it a joke? She wants to sell the land to Penny with no dirt in it?"

Charlotte shook her head. "That's what was fishy about Bucky's death."

"What? A hole?"

"The fact that Stephanie was involved. Things never feel quite right when she's involved."

Declan nodded. "This, I know."

CHAPTER THIRTY

Stephanie heard the front door of her law storefront open and stood to walk from her office into the small lobby. Stopping outside her office door, she smiled upon seeing her visitor, a small, nervous-looking older woman.

"Cora. What a surprise."

Cora Bloom's jaw clenched. "We need to talk."

"No, we don't. You need to start packing for New England. Those grandkids aren't going to spoil themselves now, are they?"

Cora took a step forward. "You stole the land from Bucky."

"Stole the land? I did no such thing. He sold it to me, fair and square. I have all the paperwork to prove it."

"You tricked him somehow."

"*Tricked* is a subjective term."

"That's why you were watching me. I figured it out. It's why you hounded me night and day. You didn't want me to stop the sale."

"Yes. Your charming company was just a bonus."

"You blocked my lawyer's calls."

Stephanie nodded. "That reminds me. He tried to reach you on your landline, too, but your housekeeper thought five hundred dollars was more important than relaying the message to you. Her loyalties were so easily bought. You might want to rethink taking her north with you."

Cora's face grew red, and Stephanie wondered if steam would soon leak from the woman's ears. Instead, Cora shook a tiny fist.

"You think you're so smart, but you're going to jail *with* us. That girl knows. She told me. She knows about Dallas and the potato gun."

"Girl? Who? Charlotte? Of course she does. I gave her the video of Dallas entering the building. It was only a matter of time. She's not quite as dumb as she looks. Just as boring, but not as dumb."

"You gave her a video? Why would you do that?
She's going to tell the police."

"Relax. Her evidence only incriminates Dallas. The world thinking Dallas worked alone is a good thing."

"But he'll tell. He'll tell, and then I'll be carted off to jail." Cora thrust a bony finger in Stephanie's direction. "And I'll tell them about you trying to cover it up, too."

Stephanie smiled and shook her head. "Dallas won't tell."

"He *will*. He's a child. He's an *idiot*. They'll scare him, and he'll tell." Cora's eyes welled with tears.

"Are you crying?" Stephanie walked to Cora and put her arm around the woman's shoulder, guiding her toward the door. "He won't tell. And without Dallas, they've got nothing except the strong suspicion that Dallas knocked Bucky over with a potato."

"You think they can't find him at school?"

Stephanie tapped her finger on the end of Cora's nose. "He's not at school, silly."

"Then where—"

Cora stopped and rotated to face Stephanie, her eyes as large as fried eggs. "Are you saying—"

Stephanie placed her hand on the small of Cora's back, opened the front door, and eased her forward into the Florida sun.

"I'm saying you have nothing to worry about from Dallas. And as long as you pay my last invoice and keep your mouth shut, you have nothing to worry about from me, either."

"Are you threatening to kill me?"

"No. I'm threatening to send a collection agency after you. I take my invoices very seriously."

Cora's lips pressed into a thin white line as she stared into Stephanie's eyes, shaking. "You're saying I have nothing to worry about?"

Stephanie gently gripped Cora's upper arm. "I'm saying you'll never have to think about Charity, or Dallas, or even Bucky again."

Cora sighed and nodded before shuffling toward her car. At her car door, she looked back.

"You won't come after me?"

Stephanie squinted at her. "Cora. I thought we were on the same page. Do I need to rethink things?"

Cora shook her head. "I'm leaving. The check will be in the mail seconds after I get home."

"Perfect. Tell your friends that if they need a lawyer, I'm here."

Cora slipped into her car and drove away as Stephanie waved from her office doorstep.

"Bye, now."

Stephanie returned to her office and sat at her desk, surveying the seventeen Teddy bears who stared back at her like a college lecture audience.

It hadn't seemed right to leave them in the trash bags.

"Well, I think we're done, boys," she said, grabbing her phone from the desk.

She dialed.

"It's done," she said when the ringing ended.

"Good. I'll send you the information you need to send me the money after you sell the land," said her mother, Jamie.

"Less my commission."

"Of course."

"And *my* loose end?"

"Tied."

"I don't want to hear how it happened, mother."

Jamie laughed.

"Oh, sweetheart. You *are* my daughter."

~~ THE END ~~

WANT SOME MORE? FREE PREVIEW!

If you liked this book, read on for a preview of the next Pineapple Port Mystery AND the Shee McQueen Mystery-Thriller Series (which shares characters with the Pineapple Port world!)

THANK YOU!

Thank you for reading! If you enjoyed this book, please swing back to Amazon and leave me a review — even short reviews help authors like me find new fans!

GET A FREE STORY

Find out about Amy's latest releases and get a free story by joining her newsletter! http://www.AmyVansant.com

ABOUT THE AUTHOR

USA Today and Wall Street Journal bestselling author Amy Vansant has written over 20 books, including the fun, thrilling Shee McQueen series, the rollicking, twisty Pineapple Port Mysteries, and the action-packed Kilty urban fantasies. Throw in a couple romances and a YA fantasy for her nieces...

Amy specializes in fun, exciting reads with plenty of laughs and action -- she tried to write serious books, but they always ended up full of jokes, so she gave up.

Amy lives in Jupiter, Florida with her muse/husband a goony Bordoodle named Archer.

BOOKS BY AMY VANSANT

Pineapple Port Mysteries
Funny, clean & full of unforgettable characters
Shee McQueen Mystery-Thrillers
Action-packed, fun romantic mystery-thrillers
Kilty Urban Fantasy/Romantic Suspense
Action-packed romantic suspense/urban fantasy
Slightly Romantic Comedies
Classic romantic romps
The Magicatory
Middle-grade fantasy

FREE PREVIEW

PINEAPPLE BEACH HOUSE

A Pineapple Port Mystery: Book Five – By Amy Vansant

A PINEAPPLE PORT MYSTERY
PINEAPPLE
Beach House
USA TODAY & WALL STREET JOURNAL BESTSELLING AUTHOR
AMY VANSANT
PINEAPPLE Beach House
AMY VANSANT

CHAPTER ONE

The tide rolled in, pushed by a tropical storm swirling off the North Carolina coast. The sea swallowed the beach, churning toward the colorfully painted houses that peered over the dunes, powerless to stop their approaching guest.

Even the most stalwart dunes meant little to an ocean, once it decided to make a house call.

The tide served as a scout for the body of the storm. The wind had yet to arrive. A chill had fallen over the barrier island, but the center of the tempest spun hundreds of miles away, idling over the Atlantic Ocean, building strength.

The man and the woman on the porch, enjoying the last of the calm weather, didn't see the tendrils of water seeping through the ground beneath the sand.

As unstoppable as an army of ants.

More powerful than a train.

The trick was patience. The water had nothing to do but *rub*. Break. Move. Fill.

Fresh, salt, brackish—it didn't matter.

Water always won.

Things rise from the ground as the water displaces them

from the places they've slept for years. Old pathway pavers, hidden by dirt for decades, shimmy their way to the surface when the water visits. Shells. Bricks. Bottles. Chunks of asphalt.

Bones.

Old and new.

Perched atop a nearby dune, a squirrel dug a hole and dropped a trophy inside.

The man and the woman didn't see this happening from their spot on the porch.

But the ghost crabs smelled it.

CHAPTER TWO

"You've got to be kidding me."

Charlotte stared at herself in the mirrored doors of Mariska's closet. She wore a yellowing cream velvet dress cinched tight at the waist with a scoop neck collar, and lace gloves.

In Florida.

Just looking at her outfit made her want to sweat.

Mariska whirled, her dark maroon cape spinning, knocking her deodorant, a hair brush and a can of shaving cream to the floor.

"Oh come on, this is fun," said Mariska, trying to bend and pick up the items that had fallen. Her dress wouldn't allow it.

Charlotte dipped to retrieve the items.

Mariska and Darla had been invited to a gothic romance book party by Veronica Deering, one of the Pineapple Port ladies. They'd insisted that Charlotte join them.

Growing up as an orphan unofficially adopted by the Pineapple Port retirement community, Charlotte had been forced or cajoled into attending hundreds of ladies' book club meetings. Most of the time she didn't mind. She knew book club meetings could be a *hoot* and were usually little more than an excuse to drink. Occasionally, it helped to actually read the featured book, but it was rarely required. Once or twice, she'd been asked to bring a potluck snack. But *no one* had ever requested she dress like undead Jane Eyre before.

"Leave it to Veronica to come up with this," said Charlotte, scratching where the lace irritated her neck.

"She's a little weird," agreed Darla.

Darla wore what Charlotte had referred to as a *Martha-Washington-as-professional-escort* ensemble. The costume shop had been woefully short on gothic romance dresses. If Veronica had requested they dress like pirate wenches, they would have had *scads* of outfits to choose from, though bare midriffs and plunging necklines in a fifty-five-plus community provided challenges of their own.

This she knew all too well.

Pirate wench outfits wouldn't do for this party, but it had still taken Charlotte ten minutes to talk Mariska out of buying a stuffed parrot to wear on her shoulder.

The three of them waddled to the lanai in their uncomfortable frocks to unveil their costumes to Mariska's husband Bob, Darla's husband, Sheriff Frank and Charlotte's boyfriend, Declan.

This was the part Charlotte had been dreading the most.

As they jostled through the sliding door that separated the lanai from the living room, Charlotte noticed the bourbons the men had poured in anticipation of their departure. The ladies' book club meant an impromptu meeting of their *Bourbon Club*, the less-veiled version of the men's "book club."

"What do you think?" Mariska asked Bob, as she completed a spin. Her cape clipped a small lamp and Charlotte dove to catch it before it crashed to the ground.

"You look like vampire Mary Poppins," said her husband. He snorted at his own joke.

Frank eyeballed Darla. "You look like the inside of a coffin."

He flinched as Darla smacked him on the shoulder.

Charlotte hooked her mouth, glaring at Declan, awaiting his verdict.

He smiled. "You look lovely..."

She scowled. "Go ahead. Finish. Get it out of your system."

"...Miss Havisham."

Charlotte sighed. She knew she *did* look like Dickens' attic-dwelling abandoned bride. "I think her dress itched less than mine," she said, clawing again at her irritated neck.

Mariska shook a finger at Bob. "Don't drink too much. We don't want to come home to a bunch of idiots."

The three men looked at each other as if they couldn't imagine what she meant.

Assured no compliments would be forthcoming, the ladies shuffled toward the front door. Charlotte exited first, and then turned in time to watch Mariska forcibly jerk Darla and her impressive poofs through the doorframe.

"A few more ruffles and you would have had to grease me like a pig," said Darla.

Charlotte continued down the driveway, only to find herself confronted by Mariska's Volkswagen Bug. She put her hands on her hips and considered the physics of the task that lay before them.

"We're going to look like clowns stuffing ourselves in that thing."

"Let's take the golf cart," suggested Darla.

"The golf cart? That's even *smaller*," said Mariska.

"Yeah, but all our dangly bits can hang over the edges."

"Don't they always?" asked Mariska.

The two older ladies burst into giggles.

Charlotte frowned at the golf cart and decided there was *some* logic to Mariska's plan. She waddled to it.

They piled onto the cart, Mariska wedged behind the wheel with Darla beside her on the front bench. Charlotte, as usual, sat in the reverse rumble seat, clinging to the framework like a koala in a eucalyptus tree during a hurricane.

Mariska backed out of the driveway as if she were being chased by a mob of angry zombies, paused long enough for Charlotte to wrap her arm snake-like around the roof pole, and then stomped on the pedal.

Charlotte's knuckles turned white. Back when her real grandmother died and Mariska explained that she and the rest of the Pineapple Port retirement community would be raising her, she never dreamed how harrowing growing up in a fifty-five-plus neighborhood would be.

Mariska's cape unfurled and fluttered across Charlotte's face, slapping her as if demanding a duel. She wrestled it down and braced her feet as Mariska rolled left.

Veronica lived in the older part of Pineapple Port, but it didn't take long to arrive with Lead Foot at the wheel. Mariska screeched to a halt behind several other carts and cars. No matter how fast Mariska had driven, it appeared that stuffing their bodies into their costumes had still left them fashionably late.

The ladies piled from the golf cart and toddled to the house, muttering beneath their breaths as they repeatedly stepped on their own, and each other's, skirts.

Hostess Veronica Deering opened her door before they could knock. She was a tall woman with black hair and a matching skin-tight gown that made her look like Dracula's mistress. She grinned upon seeing them.

"Ladies, how good of you to come."

Mariska and Darla said their hellos. Charlotte also returned the greeting, but felt her smile fading as her attention locked on Veronica's ruby red lips.

Something about her shade of lipstick seemed *off*.

Too red? Too shiny?

Mariska noticed as well, gushing over the lip gloss. "Your lipstick almost looks like wet blood, but in a *good* way."

"You're too funny," said Veronica, chortling as she led them into the house. If she was offended by the comparison of her lip gloss to bodily fluids, she didn't show it. There was no denying that Mariska had perfectly articulated what Charlotte had been thinking.

The center island of Veronica's kitchen was laden with snacks. Mariska and Darla headed toward them as if pulled by magnets.

"I hope the deviled eggs aren't all gone," mumbled Mariska, straining to see.

A man nodded at Charlotte and she smiled. He licked his lips, gazing at her as if he were starving and she was a juicy hamburger.

Hm. Disturbing.

Her progress toward the island grew slower and she scanned the room, carefully avoiding eye contact with the leering man.

Oh no.

All the party guests appeared as if they'd just awoken from their coffins. Women in dresses with draping sleeves chatted with men in leather pants and frilly white shirts. *Seventy-year-old men in leather pants.* Several of the men wore eyeliner.

Charlotte scooted to Darla's side. "Notice anything odd about this party?"

"Hm?" grunted Darla, a piece of pepperoni hanging from her lip for a second before her tongue swept it to safety.

"Look."

Charlotte grabbed Darla's head and pointed her gaze toward a man and a woman on Veronica's lanai. The man was licking the woman's neck.

Darla's eyes grew wide. "What in the name of fat Elvis are *they* doin'?"

Charlotte leaned past Darla to tug on Mariska's sleeve.

"Oh, Charlotte. You have to try this punch. It has the strangest consistency and it's a little salty, but—"

"*Mariska,*" Charlotte hissed. "What kind of party did you say this is?"

"Gothic romance?"

"What did Veronica call it, *exactly*?"

Mariska pursed her lips. "Um...just what I said. A Goth party."

Charlotte closed her eyes and groaned.

A steel-haired woman in a knee brace hobbled by sporting five earring piercings, a nose ring, a lip bolt and what looked like a silver snake weaving through her eyebrow.

Darla gasped.

"Not something you see every day," agreed Charlotte.

"It's her *knee*."

Something about Darla's comment struck Charlotte as odd. "Wait... She just walked by with all those piercing and you gasped at her knee brace?"

Darla nodded. "You have to remove everything metal for an MRI. It must have taken her a *year* to get ready for it."

"And they're just the piercings we can *see*," said Mariska. She popped a cheese square into her mouth and stared at the crowd. "It looks like they're remaking the Golden Girls using the cast of the Addams Family."

Charlotte felt something brush her neck and jumped, yipping like a Yorkshire terrier. She whirled to find a tall, thin old man behind her, smirking. Slapping her hand to her neck, she felt *moisture*.

"Did you just lick my neck?" she asked, horrified.

His smile broadened, revealing what looked like pointy, filed-down dentures.

"Delicious," he said, his eyes flashing with import.

The man leaned towards her again and she put her hand on his chest to stop his progress. She stared into his eyes.

"Buddy, you lick me again and I'll drive a *porterhouse* steak through your heart. Believe me, it takes a lot longer to die that way."

The man blanched and wandered away.

Charlotte turned to Mariska and Darla.

"We're out of here," she said, circling her finger in the air above her head.

Darla and Mariska gathered a few extra snacks from the spread and followed her lead to the door.

"Are you leaving?" asked Veronica, touching Mariska's arm as she passed.

Mariska nodded. "There's been a mistake, Ronnie. I thought this was a *book* club."

Veronica gaped. "A *book club*? You know, I thought it was strange when you asked to come. What did you think *light S & M* meant on the invite?"

Mariska shrugged. "Snacks and meats?"

"Weirdos!" called Darla from the entrance landing. She leaned in and yanked Mariska outside.

Charlotte flashed Veronica an apologetic smile and hurried after the others.

The three of them crowded back into the golf cart and Mariska hit the gas.

"Snacks and meats?" screamed Charlotte from the back.

Mariska glanced back at her. "How was I supposed to know that sort of thing was going on in Pineapple Port?"

"No telling the men. I'll never hear the end of it," said Darla.

Mariska nodded. "Absolutely. No telling."

Charlotte squelched her rising giggles and tried to remain quiet.

She couldn't *wait* to get back and tell Declan.

ANOTHER FREE PREVIEW!

THE GIRL WHO WANTS

A Shee McQueen Mystery-Thriller by Amy Vansant

CHAPTER ONE

Three Weeks Ago, Nashua, New Hampshire.

Shee realized her mistake the moment her feet left the grass.

He's enormous.

She'd watched him drop from the side window of the house. He landed four feet from where she stood, and still, her brain refused to register the warning signs. The nose, big and lumpy as breadfruit, the forehead some beach town could use as a jetty if they buried him to his neck...

His knees bent to absorb his weight and *her* brain thought, *got you.*

Her brain couldn't be bothered with simple math: *Giant, plus Shee, equals Pain.*

Instead, she jumped to tackle him, dangling airborne as his knees straightened and the *pet the rabbit* bastard stood to his full height.

Crap.

The math added up pretty quickly after that.

Hovering like Superman mid-flight, there wasn't much she

could do to change her disastrous trajectory. She'd *felt* like a superhero when she left the ground. Now, she felt more like a Canada goose staring into the propellers of Captain Sully's Airbus A320.

She might take down the plane, but it was going to *hurt.*

Frankenjerk turned toward her at the same moment she plowed into him. She clamped her arms around his waist like a little girl hugging a redwood. Lurch returned the embrace, twisting her to the ground. Her back hit the dirt and air burst from her lungs like a double shotgun blast.

Ow.

Wheezing, she punched upward, striking Beardless Hagrid in the throat.

That didn't go over well.

Grabbing her shoulder with one hand, Dickasaurus flipped her on her stomach like a sausage link, slipped his hand under her chin and pressed his forearm against her windpipe.

The only air she'd gulped before he cut her supply stank of damp armpit. He'd tucked her cranium in his arm crotch, much like the famous noggin-less horseman once held his severed head. Fireworks exploded in the dark behind her eyes.

That's when a thought occurred to her.

I haven't been home in fifteen years.

What if she died in Gigantor's armpit? Would her father even know?

Has it really been that long?

Flopping like a landed fish, she forced her assailant to adjust his hold and sucked a breath as she flipped on her back. Spittle glistened on his lips, his brow furrowed as if she'd asked him to read a paragraph of big-boy words.

His nostrils flared like the Holland Tunnel.

There's an idea.

Making a V with her fingers, Shee thrust upward, stabbing into his nose, straining to reach his tiny brain.

Goliath roared. Jerking back, he grabbed her arm to unplug her fingers from his nose socket. She whipped away her limb before he had a good grip, fearing he'd snap her bones with his

Godzilla paws.

Kneeling before her, he clamped both hands over his face, cursing as blood seeped from behind his fingers.

Shee's gaze didn't linger on that mess. Her focus fell to his crotch, hovering a foot above her feet, protected by nothing but a thin pair of oversized sweatpants.

Scrambled eggs, sir?

She kicked.

He howled.

Shee scuttled back like a crab, found her feet and snatched her gun from her side. The gun she should have pulled *before* trying to tackle the Empire State Building.

"Move a muscle and I'll aerate you," she said. She always liked that line.

The golem growled, but remained on the ground like a good dog, cradling his family jewels.

Shee's partner in this manhunt, a local cop easier on the eyes than he was useful, rounded the corner and drew his own weapon.

She smiled and holstered the gun he'd lent her. Unknowingly.

"Glad you could make it."

Her portion of the operation accomplished, she headed toward the car as more officers swarmed the scene.

"Shee, where are you going?" called the cop.

She stopped and turned.

"Home, I think."

His gaze dropped to her hip.

"Is that my gun?"

Made in United States
Troutdale, OR
10/20/2023

13862905R00106